Blood Law

by Philip J. Axiom

© 2015 Philip J. Axiom

Back ground

      The world around us seems simple. We live based on what we know and assume that is all there is. We master the world. Then something new comes into our world. All of a sudden new rules appear, new people, new secrets, and new revelations. It's almost like learning life over but this time adding something new, like when a teacher brings stuff up you forgot from middle school. You remember the idea but this time it makes sense. Before it was a fuzzy idea you struggled with. Now you see it as if it was part of you all along. Like it was never forgotten. Processing from here is similar. But a question should be asked. If you know something to be true, can you look at it to find a different truth? Can what you grow up with, which brings warmth and comfort, bring reality that you can't turn from?

Childhood

      Each day comes and goes; new people are born and grow, while other people's genes tell them to stop. Another birthday passes as we happily blow out each candle and blow through another day closer to death. New babies come into this world full of life with soft bodies; then their ancestors leave wrinkled and beaten, everyone standing around graves remembering their good, their bad. How many years a person has, no one knows, we only remember that person until that memory dies with them. Then that person doesn't exit, erased from history when all men forget their memories. Men lived and died trying to find a way to add days to their lives. Immortality, no one really knows what that means but they try to get it anyways even if they don't know the price it costs.

      Well it's been a month at this new school. We should be here until we are 20; 365 days a year, 7 days a week, 24 hours a day. We all came to this place after elementary school. We spent hours in these pods walking around in some virtual world learning how to live in the real one, this one, the only one they said matters. See when you are born, well I don't really know what happens, but you just kind of wake up in this place. The virtual world, I guess. I can't remember how I got there or why or when it started. But you just wake up and you can already speak the main standard language. You already know how to walk and talk, eat, sleep. Funny thing is, you don't remember learning these things, you just know them. Just like you know this world is not real, but they told us that and they explained it to us; how we are hooked up to an electric exoskeleton that you move around in it and it keeps you up right while copying your moves in the virtual world.

While we lived in this world, we were taught everything we needed. See you spend so much time in an empty white plane; it's like an endless white floor. There's this teacher, it's really a computer, and the teacher teaches you Math and English. As the teacher teaches us words, equations, graphs and charts, all fly in the air. It's like they were suspended on a wall but there isn't a wall there; almost like the wall was clear. When it was time to learn science you were put in a lab with everything you needed to learn. Of course it was a virtual but it felt like you could actually touch the tools and move things around. We had cars that we learned to dismantle; always with a lesson on how it works by the teacher. When it was time for biology and anatomy, we did "live dissections" where the teacher taught us our directions and we used virtual tools to cut open a frog or cow, sometimes it was a human and we would learn everything we could.

	You know, everyone loved history time. See wherever you went was a clock that followed you over your head. It counted telling you the time and date and how long you had before something started and stopped. We didn't know what time it was in the real world. But you had so many hours a day to sleep, and it was very precise. You had so many hours to learn, Math, English, science and so on. Then you had so many hours in history. See, a bell rang every time something new came and something was over. When it came time for history the world around you changed.

	You started with this small kingdom called Babylon. They started writing here in some place out between seven hills; around them all over the world where these barbarian tribes that had a culture of severity. The land of Babylon was the only nation that was civilized. Then one king came to power, united the land, and helped build the mighty city-state. He protected it from invaders but one day he was assassinated. After him, this leader called Caesar comes to power, changed the kingdom and used marvel and limestone, and changed the military. After that, he expanded our kingdom into an empire across the world and united it into one great world. After that, you see the changes as people, leader, discoveries and technology changes. The only thing important you learn as far as history goes is just small rebellions and movements that the old barbarian people tried to make. They are always doing something and they never seem too die out. They tried to have their ideas like people are individuals and we should be able to say and think what we want. Of course, the teacher explained to us how these ideas are dangerous and how we will offend people and that's not nice or how ideas like morals and rights are wrong. The teacher has a scripted laugh at this and says the only thing right and wrong is what our law says. It's supposed to be safer and more peaceful that way.

    The reason why history is every one's favorite is because you get to walk around and talk to people; both on the streets and people in power. You can see all the architecture and work with the people. In some time periods, you have the option of fighting in the army and protecting famous people. It's always fun to go around and read the classic books or go to a music performance from different time periods and see the changes.

    We never really meet any real people until a week before we had to leave; or at least they said it was a week. The bell rang and we ended up appearing in this bar looking place with other people and we were told that they were real. You could tell the difference right away, they talked without being choppy and conversations weren't always predictable and didn't sound rehearsed.

    I won't forget the first day coming to this school. The clock had a countdown going off the last week and it was finally up. I was in a blank room sitting in a chair while the teacher congratulated me, telling me what to expect. Then I felt myself falling and the exoskeleton hit the bottom of the pod. It opens and a helmet pulled itself off my head. I was in a cylinder with lights all around me. The skeleton was holding me up. As it was opening it gave off a puff of steam and the light in the pod dimmed. There where rows and rows of pods all lined up. There was a path between each row and above us were another set of pods and rows and above that another. Everyone poked their heads out and looked for some kind of direction. Then a light shinned on the paths in the shape of an arrow flashing and running down the paths telling us where to go; we were all wearing stretchy blue suits that fitted our whole body skintight.

Some people took their first steps on the path and followed the arrows. I looked down at the floor, lifted my foot off the padding of the exoskeleton, and placed it on the real solid ground for the first time. I thought maybe it would feel different or I might not be strong enough to stand, but it was just the same as walking in the pod. My foot went forward and my body lifted from the skeleton then my other foot went forward. I got into line with everyone else following the arrows and walked out of this building. When I took my first steps outside, I felt the nature sunlight hit me. They replicated it very well in the virtual world. The air felt clean and free. Inside when you breathe, everything was stuffy but it wasn't out here.

When we came outside some fences kept us in lines and we went into another line. We came into another building; this one was smaller and inside was just small changing rooms. By the door was a dispenser with a sign saying free clothes. Everyone walked over grabbed the clothes then went to go change. After that, we left the building and went up to some buses that took us to this school.

I remember coming and seeing the school grounds. We came in through a gate down the road in the woods. By the entrance, there were several buildings huddled around a small fenced area. Later I found out that this was where all the adults lived. They had everything they needed, away from the rest of the school. We drove pass these buildings down a long strip of road; through more woods. In the middle of the school, ground was where the rest of the buildings were. In the center was a courtyard, around that were several buildings for classes, one building for languages arts; one for math, and one for each of the sciences, biology, physics, chemistry, robots, and computers. They had the building mixed in with the dorms along with other buildings.

    South was for every sport that could be played outside, with indoor courts for other sports all around the main gym. Off to the side of this was the entertainment center where people gathered for different events. To the north of all the buildings was the music center. Our dorms were mixed in between all the school buildings and all around there were small stores and restaurants. We weren't going anywhere soon, so they made sure we had everything we needed to live here and prepare us for when we leave. They had small factories around where different things were made. Once a week some trucks would come in to the school grounds to deliver supplies to some of the buildings that made stuff. Raw material would come in and if there were extra manufactured stuff, which there always was, the trucks would take it off somewhere.

    Everyone here mainly spent their time at restaurants. The best restaurant was the one across from the music center, the Red Note. Everyone wanted to go there. Whenever you walked by and the doors were opened when the sounds blasted out and you just felt like you belonged. In order to get in you had to pay just to reserve a day to eat there and pay a good price just to reserve a seat, not including a meal. I went there one time, the tables were all set around a dancing floor, off to the left was a bar place. To the right, tables to eat and straight ahead when you walked in was a beautiful stage with live music playing every day. Around the school grounds was a forest; we were told that an electric fence was out there somewhere. I never saw it and no one ever talked about it. Some people think it's a myth to keep people from trying to run away.

    Either way, in order to live here, we actually have to save and use money. In the virtual world whenever we were in history, depending on the time period, we used different kinds of currency. We started off learning how to value things with the old forms of bartering different goods with virtual people. As the time period changed, we started using different kinds of coins made of various kinds of metals. We learned how to value things based off of purity of the metal. Then we started using checks and then paper notes based off of a standard. We used many different things and they explained it to us why each of them was valuable. The real life currency we used was different. For some reason they never showed us or talked to us about it. It wasn't a coin but it was shaped like one. It was a container of some kind and inside of it was dark maroon; about the size of two dimes and had a raised drop printed on one side with an official marking on the other. When I had first seen it, I noticed right away that the coin shaped container itself was clear silicon; it was only thick enough to protect whatever was inside. What was on the inside, I'm not sure. At first I thought maybe it was some kind of emerald or maybe copper mixed with maybe tungsten. It stayed perfectly rock solid in the silicon except one time when I found a defected one. It weighed less than the other ones and I kept on shaking it around and at one point; it started to seem like a liquid. I kept shaking it and I thought for a moment that it split into layers. But either way the coin container its self had 8 ounces printed on it.

***

  It's been a month at this school; we were all outside by the football field, behind one of the bleachers was where the tree was. I was sitting up against the bleachers with Bryan. He was fidgety and chewing on some plant. Over leaning by the tree was Jesse standing perfectly still. Between him and us was Nick sitting on the ground also chewing. Over looking away from us was Max leaning against the side of the bleacher.
  "All I'm saying is we need to be spot on later. We have one shot at playing in the Red Note." Bryan spoke with a sharp enthusiasm.
  "Guys, stop obsessing over this. We got it." Nick stood up and walked over to Jesse. "We have an amazing drummer, the one that every music teacher brags about." He threw his

arm around Jesse and walked him over to us. He pointed to Bryan, "Now who is ever going to forget these solos from our piano." Bryan wanted to smile but held it in. Nick pointed to me, "Of course all our harmony just flows from our guitarist with all those chords with the voicing leadings just so right."

Bryan spoke almost stumbling over his words, "and only if we had a base that could stay on rhythm."

Nick smiled, "yes it doesn't help with some piano player trying to play off beat" everyone chuckled. Nick turned his body while having Jesse hold his weight leaning back, "and who could ever forget that angelic voice from the man who brought us together." Max was still standing over at the end of the bleachers not responding.

Bryan looked over at Jesse, "you think he's ok?"

Jesse shrugged, "it's his last year here. He might have that senior fear."

Nick spit out some plant and placed some new leaves in his mouth, "come on, he can't be scared. How could he, if any one's going to make it in this world it's him for sure."

Bryan stood up cuffing his hands together to Nick asking for more leaves, "All the seniors get it. It's a big step, he's about to be an adult soon."

Max turned and said, "I can hear every word you guys are saying."

Bryan smiled, "see he's fine."

Max walked over to them. "You guys can't forget we are getting someone new to join us. Things might change when he's with us." He looked around at all of us then paused, "what are you guys chewing?"

Nick tried being slick and spit it out while Bryan tried hiding the leaves in his mouth. Bryan answered, "Nothing."

"I told you guys to stop chewing those leaves. If any of the medical staff finds out that you guys are chewing you are going to be taken away." Max walked over to them and held out his hand. Bryan spit out the leaves in his hand, and then he turned to Nick.

"I already spit it out."

Max threw the leaves on the ground; "I should have some more *fixer sticks* in my room. What classes do you guys have next?"

Bryan answered, "We have gym."

"All of you?"

"Yea."

Max thought for a moment, "This is bad. When they draw in blood they are going to find out someone in your gym group has been chewing. You guys better hope you can clean your system out before they draw that blood in."

Nick jumped in, "you can bring us some sticks?"

"I would but I'm on the other side of the school grounds. If you guys can get some from anyone else, try to. You guys have to stop getting attention. It's not good to have attention on you especially not like that. You guys should start listening to me, you are going to pay for it one day." everyone was silent. Max sighed, "well hurry up and get to class I'll find someone to bring you some fixer stick. Take the long route today, get your blood flowing and don't be late for the rest of the week or they will start keeping an eye on you." Max walked away.

Bryan turned to Nick, "Man why is it he is always uptight about this stuff? If we get some fixer sticks, it will help clear out blood and they will never know. It's that easy."

Jesse turned to him and said, "No it doesn't clear your blood. It makes you generate more blood. All it will do is water down the leaves in your system. They could still detect it and the longer you guys go before eating one the more time it will take before it starts working."

Everyone started walking over to the gym together. We did what Max said and took the long way to gym arriving 5 minute late. We entered the front doors of the training gym and our gym trainer stared us down as we walked in. The man spoke with a piercingly loud voice, "Where have you guys been? You're late! Hurry up and get in the changing room, you all have 3 minutes!"

We all ran to the changing room while everyone in the gym laughed at us for getting yelled at. We went into the rooms and headed to our lockers. We put our fingers on lock pads and the lock scanned our fingers. The locks opened and we all started changing. Bryan called us, "Hey, Max works fast, there are five sticks in here." he showed us the sticks; they were blue sticks that almost looked like thin pieces of celery.

Jesse was stiffly putting on his pants, "well you guys better hurry up and eat them." Our gym clothes were all the same. They were gray short sleeve under armor with small amounts of padding, around different parts of the under armor where some small plastic tubes. We also had black shorts with shoes that automatically sense the ground and could change from running shoes into cleats.

We all walked out of the changing room and our gym trainer was standing there. "Hurry up, get out on that court!"

We went and did our normal warm up routine; hundred pushups with weights on our back, sit ups, pull-ups and 10 laps around the gym equaling 2 miles. After we finished the trainer called us over. "Why are you guys late?" the trainer paused as if expecting an answer. Out of experience, we all knew he didn't want one. "You all knew that this is the most important class!" Everyone else in the gym was lined up on the side of the room all trying to hold in a laugh. "This class was to help prepare you just in case you ever have to be called to help exterminate any of those barbarian rebels! That is one of the greatest things you could ever do. Being drafted is an honor. At any time anyone of you could be called to arms. No one has ever made it back alive and they die honoring our great empire. Now go get into line and I don't want to see you guys ever coming late to this class again!"

We all sprinted back to the line and the teacher walked up and down the line. "Now that you have been undergoing conditioning for the last few months, it's time to move on to the next part of the class. Every day when you walk in here a few kids will have to come to help set up; preferably early." The man looked at us at the end of the line. Everyone chuckled.

"Did I say you could laugh?" Everyone quickly stopped. "Each morning there will be an obstacle cores. It will be changed once every three classes and become progressively hard. One third of you will be running the obstacle courses while another third works on fighting skills and the last portion will be continuing our normal body training. The class will be split into three parts and everyone will rotate according to my word. Understood?"

Everyone stood up tall and simultaneously said, "Yes sir!"

"Good, now go finish off the rest of your exercises for the day and wait for the medical person to come, Dismissed." Everyone then walked from the line and went back to work out. I walked over to get some water. Nick was standing over by the water fountain by the doors to the gym. He was off to the side of the fountain catching his breath. I walked over to get some water and said, "Are you feeling alright."

"Not sure, I haven't felt like this since we started conditioning."

"Well what's wrong with you?"

"Not sure. I just feel like I can't breathe that well."

I looked over my shoulder then back at him, "well come on. Better hope that the teacher doesn't see you or he will get up in your face. After this class, you should probably go see the nurse. Come on." I put my hand on his shoulder and we started jogging off.

After class, the medical person came and started setting up by the door. The medical person was always a student from the upper class who was picked to become a doctor. This student was a girl wearing a mask, blue gloves, a hair net and a white apron. She had golden hair and blue eyes. The line was formed quickly when she walked into the room. Some of the guys even stood around her and she had to tell them to get into line. Bryan and Nick tried to be last in line and Jesse and I were in front of them. The line went by fast and everyone quickly saw the girl and then headed for the changing room.

When it came time for Jesse's turn, the room was almost empty.

The girl looked at us and said, "Next." She looked at the clock, "you guys must be upset being stuck at the back of the line, and it's cutting into your lunch time. Sorry about that."

Bryan smiled, "we are always late anyway."

"Really? Even on a day like today? I heard some of the sophomores are learning to cook ribs again. This should be something, right?"

Jesse walked up first and she pointed at the chair that was abnormally tall so Jesse could sit on. Nick said, "Well if they are making it that might be a bad thing."

"Ha yea, who knows what their special sauce is."

Jesse said, "Yea, I think I will pass on the ribs for today. Thanks guys." The girl started checking his reflexes.

Bryan and Nick walked up to the chair, "so what year are you in?"

"I'm a senior"

Nick and Bryan both looked at each other. Nick continued the conversation; "Well the line usually moves slower than this. You must have had practice."

"I've done it plenty of times. I don't think I ever had your group before. It's annoying having all these guys trying to flirt with you."

Bryan chuckled, "I know what you mean and the ladies do the same to me sometimes."

Jesse smiled on the chair and let out a short laugh under his breath. "O so I guess you know how I feel then." The girl finished drawing Jesse's blood. "Who's next?"

Bryan and Nick looked at each other. I walked over to the chair, "I am. I'll go."

Bryan moved aside so I could sit then continued talking, "Yea, I guess I do then. Especially when they all keep trying to use cheesy pick up lines… man I hate that."

She finished checking on my reflexes and pulled out a clean needle. She attached it to a thin plastic tube and started to draw blood. I watched as the flow of blood went from the needle down the tube and then in to a special container where everyone else's blood was. After she finished, I stood up from the seat and started to walk over where Jesse was waiting off to the side.

The girl called me, "Hey take some of these blood stimulating sticks. It's important that your blood levels stay up." she handed me a bundle of them.

Nick tapped Bryan and tried to whisper, "she comes with free fixer sticks."

Jesse walked over and grabbed one, then turned to the girl, "Where does our blood go after it's been drawn?" He then placed a small part of the stick in his mouth and took a small bit.

"It goes off of the school grounds to be used for different needs."

"Like what?"

"I don't really know. I guess it goes off and is used to help the troops fight the barbarians or they keep it in hospitals for emergencies." Jesse knotted his hand and we both walked over to the changing rooms. Jesse opened the door for me; as soon as I was inside he closed the door and said, "So you think they will get her to meet them later?"

I smiled, "Well the way they are trying I'm surprised she even kept the conversation going. She's probably just going to give them hope and then leave them hanging if they even manage to get anywhere." We started changing.

"It's funny how hard they are trying."

"Ha, Yea, I keep forgetting how bad they are with the ladies."

The door opened; Nick and Bryan stepped into the room. Jesse turned around, "how did it go?"

Bryan had a smile; "she said she wouldn't mind meeting up with us later today."

I looked at Jesse then said, "Oh really? Where are you, two meeting?"

Bryan looked at Nick whose face was red with anger, "the Red Note. I told her I was playing there today and she said she would come and see me perform." Bryan had a large smile on his face.

Nick looked over at him, "she would see us perform… if you didn't hog all the attention all the time that conversation would have been different."

"It would have been boring for her." They both walked over to get changed "And I wasn't hogging the attention. You had plenty of time to make a move and you didn't. So someone had to keep her company and I guess that was me." Nick slammed his locker and went over by the exit. We all followed him shortly.

We only had 40 minutes left for lunch. We walked around trying to find a good place to eat. Bryan wanted tacos while Nick wanted steak. Then Bryan wanted lasagna while Nick wanted ribs. After wasting 20 minutes, we saw max sitting alone in a window. We went over and filled the seats around him. He didn't pay attention to us. Instead he had earpieces on listening to music while staring into his coffee. The waiter who already served max before came back, "do you need something else or will the coffee be enough?"

Max looked up, "yes, what do you guys want?" We all glanced over the menu and shouted orders at the waiter. He jotted them all down and walked off. When he was gone Max looked up from his coffee again. He took a small silver disk from his ear. He held the earpiece in his hand and turned to us, "So did they draw blood?"

Nick answered, "Yes they did, but, it wasn't as bad as we thought it would be."

Bryan jumped in, "It wasn't, it was actually quicker than normal, or at least it felt that way."

Jesse smiled briefly. Max looked at him and then at me, "what did he find so funny?"

I looked over at Jesse then back at Max, "Well, they tried to pick up the medical person there."

Max looked at them, "Wow, I'm not surprised. So she didn't notice anything?"

Bryan smiled, "well she noticed something."

Max chuckled and shook his head, "I meant about your blood."

The waiter came back with the food and everyone stopped talking. The waiter had on a mechanical skeleton around his hands, his palm was flat and he had a large tray of food over his head. "All right, here you all go." the waiter spun the tray on the mechanical skeleton; with his other hand he stretched out his fingers and the skeleton stretched out so he could grab the food. When he was done he held his palm off to the side. The tray was almost the size of his torso.

As the waiter walked away, Jesse was placing a napkin on his lap, then another one partially in his shirt. "It was just a blood collection. No test was done."

Max sipped his coffee and turned to Jesse, "and you are sure?" Jesse knotted his head, and then turned to take a bite. "You guys are lucky. They won't know it's you if they find anything." Everyone was eating trying not to make eye contact. Max looked around at us, "You guys have to try and keep it cool. When I leave, you guys better make it out this school to live." Everyone stopped eating for a moment.

We looked around at each other then Bryan broke the silence, "what do you mean make it out to live?"

Max sipped his Coffee, "It's an expression. I'm just saying you guys need to keep it cool." Everyone went back to eating, "so we need to meet by 5; right after your last class for practice."

Jesse swallowed, wiped his mouth and spoke; "We aren't giving permission to enter the Red Note until 8."

Max knotted, "Don't forget, we still have to break in the new guy."

Nick finished his plate, "I forgot about him. What's his name?"

Bryan started talking with his mouth full, "I think it's Phil Mabone"

Jesse corrected him, "Dill Maborn."

Max smiled, "you guys should be paying attention to these things. The people you see around you are the people you're stuck with until you leave."

Nick blurted out; "Yea but at least we will be together for years after this, playing music." Everyone smiled and laughed. Nick and Bryan started making jokes back and forth. As soon as Nick made that remark, Max turned away from us and looked out the window.

After a moment a bell rang, this one was the one that rings all over the school just like the one in the virtual world. Everyone stood up from the table. Max got up last, "what class are you all going to?"

Jesse looked like he was thinking; "We all have different classes now."

Max looked at me, "Where are you going?"

I thought for a moment, "Today is Thursday?"

Everyone chuckled except max, "yes."

"Not sure."

"And what's your last class?

"Should be Advising"

Max looked at the others and told them as we walked out the building, "Well make sure you guys meet at the storage room as soon as you can. I'll tell Dill now." Everyone walked off in different directions.

I went pulling out a small glass pad. As soon as I looked at the glass screen, it lit up. The screen was transparent with lines of applications on the screen. As I walked down the street I could see my feet strolling across the floor through the screen. I looked up for a moment and saw everyone around me walking. The streets of the school had three main sections laid down by stained bricks. The middle section was the largest and it was stained blue. It was large enough for traffic to flow in two directions. There were people on electric bicycles and hover boards scarily zooming to class. The rest of the street was stained gray, with two red marking outlines for people to walk in.

I looked back down at the glass pad and tapped on one of the applications. The screen went to a loading screen; "campus help" was flashing. The screen changed and displayed several options. I tapped one of them and my schedule popped up. Through the screen I saw the street come to an intersection. I paused and looked up. Everyone was crossing the street. All the freshmen had their bags stuffed. The sophomores' bags were reasonable. The juniors' bags only had their belongings in them and carried the bag on one shoulder. All the seniors walked around with nothing on, not worried about class.

    I looked back at the screen and skimmed through the schedule. I had argumentative history. My glass pad had a small timer counting down the time I had left before getting to the next class. Three minutes, luckily the building was right around the corner and the room was on the second floor. When I got to the front doors they opened by themselves. I continued down the main lobby to an elevator. When I was three feet from the door the elevator opened and another person walked in with me. The doors closed and over the doors were digital numbers with the second and eight floors already highlighted. The elevator zoomed to the second floor and opened for me. Several people walked in and more numbers highlighted. Everyone was blocking me so the elevator wouldn't close until I was out.

    My room was on the right. Three other kids walked into the room. Mr. Galvar was standing by the door with a smile as everyone walked in. I walked into the class and he walked in a moment after. Mr. Galvar walked over to his desk and did a quick survey of the class with his eyes. He licked his lips then went to write on the board. I was sitting in the back corner. The desk had a glass panel for a surface and a metal frame with wood seats.

    Mr. Galvar turned from the board, "all right, now start with a brain storm and hand in your homework." I took out my glass pad and went through the applications. My homework was under a file in my student aid application. I tapped on it, "Essay on barbarians ideas in history," then swiped my finger over the pad; the desk lighted up with my essay. Several buttons appeared in the corner of the glass panel. I sent in the homework.

The brainstorm on the board was to write as many barbarian ideas as you could and the reasons why they were bad. Everyone in the class was silent as Mr. Galvar was at his desk looking over our homework. Every so often he would glance at us and lick his lips as if he was waiting for dinner.

I reached in my bag for a pen to write on the glass surface of the desk. The one I had was the one like everyone had; it was customized to the way I write and hold it. The pen touched the desk and my hand started forming bubbles with ideas and arguments. On the board was a timer that was connected to our desk; every second was calculated to the nearest millisecond to maximize learning. The clock was nearing the last three seconds; everyone was rushing to fit all last second ideas. When the clock went down to the last millisecond our desks froze.

Mr. Galvar stood up from his desk and walked up to the board, then faced the class. He looked over at one desk, "Martian, I don't know why you are still trying to write. Your desk won't unfreeze until I hit the button." Everyone laughed, "Now let us see what you all brain stormed." He tapped his marker to the board and someones work they had on their desk was up in front for everyone to see, exactly how it was on the desk. "Yes, Matthew, very good work. It seems you covered all the barbarian ideas and the arguments against them. Although next time, remember, a well thought out idea should be expressed in more than two well written sentences."

Mr. Galvar then went to the next person. "Jenna, this is perfect. Class, give her a loud applause." Everyone clapped, "She has all the ideas, well arguments and look here. She made some new arguments. She even has a well-constructed paragraph for each topic. Very good, just next time, try not to make your own ideas. See this argument here." he pointed, "on the barbarian idea of individualism, you put that, 'we are one nation and individuals can't run themselves as a nation.' This is nice. But see, that is not an answer that would be expect-able. See the argument I gave you here," he pointed with a smile, "that you wrote down. 'People need guidance because they are not capable of guiding themselves.' This is a proper answer. It addresses your argument and can be used to cover others."

Mr. Galvar moved onto the next person, "Timothy, very nice organizational skills. Everyone look, he applied the skills he learned from other classes very well. Each argument is well spaced out, all his writing spaces is maximized while still leaving room to identify each idea. Very nice, next time just get to the point faster and not give 300 years worth of history." Everyone chuckled again.

He called my name, "Well sir, I see you didn't quite pay attention to my lectures or studied enough for the homework." He lifted my work off the board while bringing up my essay. "See, your brain storm almost models your essay in content. They are both missing it. What you have isn't enough." He zoomed in and started reading some of my brainstorm.

"You managed to remember only 5 barbarian ideas, luckily they are the big ones; but still you lack content. See here, you have; individualism, free speech, private property, freedom and free thought.

Under free thought you put, 'we are told what's right' and leave it there. That is true but you didn't go into detail of how free thoughts are dangerous, they could lead to people getting hurt by trying something new; or how it leads to rebellion.

Under freedom you put, 'we are only allowed to do what the law says' yes but you didn't put that our law is perfect; or how freedom can lead to mistakes. There are mistakes so freedom is barbaric in nature.

One thing you forgot to mention in your thesis was a fundamental thing, if barbaric ideas exist in society then there is no unity. If no one can agree, everyone is their own person, then how can we have one idea or goal?" Mr. Galvar went on for ten minutes using my paper as a bad example to review the lesson.

When class was over I noticed several people laughing at me as I walked out the door. Most people don't get a 30 percent error on any assignment. A 10 percent error is considered poor, over 7 percent is frowned upon. I got full credit for having the formatting right, spelling, grammar, and mechanics of language. I lost 20 percent for not using enough content and 10 percent for not sticking to the prompt. As I was heading out the door I remembered hearing Mr. Galvar telling me how I got the lowest grade he ever gave in his class; the second, apparently, was an 11 percent error. Luckily he said I could re-do the grade by making up 2 new essays correctly done by the end of the week. I don't think he knew it was Thursday.

My next class was across the street in the general education building. It was a smaller building compared to the others. What was taught in here were classes that didn't fit into "important subject matters" for the majority of people to know such as law classes. A big part of the building was for the law students, probably because it seemed like almost no one took them except for a handful of people like Max.

Normally, in my schedule I would have a miscellaneous class where they just talk about general things in life that just about everyone already knew. For some reason they had everyone from my gym class this morning all together. I sat next to my friends and we all waited for a teacher to show up.

"We are probably here for some informational thing." Bryan was turned from a desk talking to Jesse.

I smiled, "O really? What made you think that?"

Nick jumped into the conversation, "But why would they pull us from our schedule? Some of the guys here should be in real academic classes."

Jesse leaned over almost as if he was being sneaking, "something happened in gym. I think it has to do with some of the broken lockers. I heard there was a fight earlier."

Bryan jerked back, "A fight? Since when do people fight here?"

Jesse shrugged, "I heard it was true, that's the only thing I could think of that happened during gym, unless-"

A man walked into the room with a large beard and glasses. The class was silent. He wasn't anyone I seen before; he walked in very elegantly, he had on a brown suit. The man walked up in front and stood with his hands behind his back; two other men wearing black suits stood on the sides of the room. Everyone was focusing forward silently.

The man's hands went forward and he had a small remote in them. He cuffed his hands in front of him and clicked a button. A slide show popped up on the board. On the board was a colorful "WARNING" sign. Under it was, "HEALTH RISK."

The man spoke with a deep soft voice, "Well good day gentlemen." He was almost motionless as he spoke. "I am the head of the school's student health department." The man's glasses were black and round; it felt like his eyes watched you at all times. "Today I have been instructed to give a health reminder to all the students."

He clicked the button and the slide changed. The slide on the board had pictures of all kinds of people with health problems. The man spoke, "what do all the people here have in common? See the man whose throat is burnt and needs medical attention? Or the person here with his veins all funny and messed up? How about this person coughing up blood? This person pale as paper and lay out on the ground. What about these others?"

The man clicked the button again; a box fizzled on the screen with large capital letters, "DRUGS." Everyone suddenly lost a lot of interest in what was coming next. Looking around the room; several people sat back looking guilty while others were bored. I quickly glanced at Bryan who was keeping a straight look. Nick seemed like he was hiding his guilt; you wouldn't be able to tell unless you knew him for a while.

The man was motionless for a moment the men who came in with him were looking around the room with their eyes scanning everything. The man with the glasses changed slides. There were several pictures of different pill bottles. The man spoke again, "now not all are bad. See some actually help us and save lives; but at the same time, they can take lives." The man paused; pure boredom filled the air with guilt and the feeling of tension.

   The man continued, "See by law it is only legal to take the right recommended amounts and only for the conditions listed. Anything outside of this is illegal and punishable by law." As the man spoke there was the knowledge that he was speaking in general terms but still sternly addressing a select few. He spoke like any other teacher but at the same time, it felt like someone disciplining us. "These under the legal instructions are safe."

   The man changed the slide; pictures of different plants filled the screen with two in particular larger than the rest. "These plants contain drugs within them, see they are unstable and unsafe for our use; because they are not standardized, using them in any way is illegal." The man changed the slide, a picture of someone smoking, sniffing and chewing on different things popped up. The man continued, "Many of these plants are illegal used. Each of these will cause additional harm in their own way along with the effect from the plants."

   The man then changed the slide, two enlarged plants from the previous slide appeared; under them were names which the man read without looking back. "This one on the right is a skavy herb as it is known. It causes: memory loss, brain damage, red eyes, and angry outbursts. In some high amounts, muscle spasms and in long term use violent behavior and often promotes criminal activity. At the same time it releases dopamine. The second image is what is known as looform leaves." I looked around the room; Bryan's face looked like he was trying to hold something in even though he was staring at the ground. Nick had his head down not listening. The man continued, "These leaves cause hallucinations, a temporary lose of the nervous system, damages brain cells, and liver failure. In some cases, it lowers the eyes' ability to water. In some cases people experience rage and violent outbursts. It releases dopamine and after long term use, leads to lose of brain functions."

The man finally moved holding his hands in front of him to the other side of the board. "As you can see, these are dangerous things. I bring this to your attention only because some areas of the campus happened to be growing some of these plants. They have been removed from the area and professionals are currently looking for more. If you find any, please leave it where you found it, notify an authority and stay away from that area. Fortunately, we are investigating people who linger around places that are suspected of growing areas to ensure the law isn't broken. That is all, have a nice day gentlemen." The man walked out of the room. The men who accompanied him followed him walking out slowly after him. The bell rang as they left the room.

The guys and I made our way to the storage building. Our room was in one of the three storage buildings around the campus and was two stories high. Inside the hallways were narrow, with just enough space to wheel a large box in one direction; along the walls were the rooms, each one varied in size depending on which part you were in. We had the largest room.

Jesse walked over to the door and unlocked it. We walked in and turned on the lights, "look they probably don't know who was using what. They might have just had a general announcement." Jesse then stayed quiet and went around the drum set in the middle of the room.

Bryan walked over to an amplifier off to the side of the drums, "They knew exactly what plants we were using." Bryan sat down at a chair next to his keyboard and played a sharp G chord.

Jesse turned quickly, "What are you doing? We have to check the sound proofing sheets before we can play."

Bryan sat leaning in his backless seat, "We did that last time. We should be ready to play."

Jesse walked around inspecting the sheets of foam on the wall, "If it's off by a little bit, then people will hear us."

The lock on the door was clicking, Max stepped in. He walked in as if he was drained of all energy. He walked over and sat down at a school desk we had in the room. Every one's face lighted up as he walked in. We all greeted him; he simply waved and lifted his head. As he sat down he finally spoke, "Did you guys check the sound proofing foam?"

Jesse walked over to the drum set, "I just finished checking it."

"Alright, Dill should be here soon. Any news?"

Bryan looked over at Nick who was getting his bass ready. "We were pulled from our class to attend an information meeting."

Max was rubbing his chin as if he was trying to give us attention. "What was it about?"

Nick continued, "There were some Looform leaves and Skavy herbs found on campus. They pulled everyone from gym to talk to us about it."

Max's face lit up with energy, "what were you guys chewing earlier today?"

Nick was silent, Max glanced back and forth between him and Bryan. Finally Bryan spoke, "Looform leaves, but just the leaves nothing else."

Max thought for a moment, "Well you said it was just a blood drawing this morning right?" Jesse nodded, "Well then, there were probably other people in your class using the other plants. Who gave the meeting?"

Jesse answered, "The head of the student health department"

"Was there anyone else?"

Everyone was thinking, I spoke up; "there were two other men in black suits."

"Did they do anything?"

"No they just stood there and watched us."

"Alright, guys what is said among us, stays between us. Understand?" Everyone nodded their heads at the familiar phrase. "The men who there were, more than likely, looking for guilty faces. If they find you doing something illegal, you will be put under the penalty of the Law. It doesn't matter who you are unless you have special privileges under certain conditions. The best thing you guys can do is avoid trouble at all cost. If you do anything out of place, cover your tracks, like it never happened. Like what we are doing. I'm paying for the rent for this place. By law, it is only used for storage and we should not be loitering here. That's why we only come here right after classes end. When people won't notice we are here.

I picked this place because there is no check in like the other ones. See, I make sure we check the sound proofing just in case anyone walks by so they won't hear us and more than likely report us. The soundproofing stuff came as a mistake out of a chemistry class. They were planning on throwing it away so it won't be missed. Once we have a registered place we can afford, we are leaving this place."

Nick sighed, "What's with all the rules? We can only spend so much time in the bathroom stalls. Why is everything so uptight?"

Bryan almost seemed suspicious at this. Jesse was curiously silent. I walked around to the guitar on the stand by the drums. Max stood up, "well here is what we do by law. If something: is unsafe that can bring harm mentally or physically; we outlaw it. If it isn't a big concern then we don't stress it. If it is a concern then those Laws are enforced more. When someone spends too much time alone, they are unproductive and tempted to break the law when people aren't around."

Jesse said, "So this is how they give people jobs then. By what they show in public and how much they can have done in secret."

Max shrugged, "that's what I've gotten out of law class."

Bryan had a confused look. "That doesn't make sense, who can-"

Max continued speaking, "there is a reason few people take law class. Just know that they are going to be watching that gym class closely. It's a good thing you guys told me. I'm going to have to spend less time away from people, even though I only want to be around you guys."

There was a knock at the door. Everyone was silent. The knocked happened again, this time more rhythmically. Max walked over and opened the door wide open. Dill walked in. "alright. Are you guys ready to practice?"

Max went over and grabbed a microphone on a stand in front of the drum set. "We were ready about five minutes ago." Dill went over, placed an amplifier on the ground. He then pulled out a guitar and started to strum simply chords. He flipped a switch on the guitar and the sound went through to the amplifier.

Everyone get into position, Dill spoke, "1, 2 1, 2 3 4." Dill started playing a song and everyone looked at him funny. After a minute of him playing the guitar by himself he stopped. Dill looked around, "what's wrong?"

Max looked at us, "I'm the one that normally counts down."

Dill shrugged "don't you guys mix things up and play whatever you want? I'm just fitting in,"

Max shook his head, "we improvise but even with that there is still an order and structure to how the group works together."

Dill shrugged again, "well do what you want."

Max turned to everyone, "1, 2, 3, 1, 2, 3, 4, 5." Jesse stiffly started up with a drum roll, Nick jumped straight into the song with the bass line. Max had his head hanging listening to the music. Bryan and I started playing along; Dill started strumming something else on his guitar. Max turned to us sticking his fist up to stop. Everyone looked at dill. Max called him, "what are you playing?"

Dill seemed uninterested, "well I looked at the song and there were all these symbols and signs. I just ignored them; the song sounds better like this."

Bryan gave him a dumb founded look, "all those symbols are there to help the song move along."

Dill shrugged, "it's not that much of a big deal."

Bryan's mouth dropped, "do you know how hard it is to get extensions beyond triads and to work together with complicated chords like this?"

Dill looked bored, "the song isn't even that good. We should play something else."

Bryan's face grew red, "Mr. Martez said that this was one of the most well constructed songs he seen in years."

Max quickly interrupted them, "Look Dill, this is what we are playing. We can't change it. I already sent the manager at the Red Note the information about us and what we are playing."

Dill shook his head and max counted down again. Everyone started up just like last time. I started playing, Bryan started; this time Dill stuck to the song. Max was hanging his head. He almost looked like he was out of energy trying to stay up by his side; his hands softly snapped keeping count. The music started to build, Max's head bobbed along. Finally Jesse did a drum roll; the music quieted down and max started singing.

Out of nowhere he seemed to be full of life; his voice rang out and his singing was perfect. Everything was perfectly balanced and the song was amazing. We played for a while then max stopped singing. Everyone took turns soloing, first it was Bryan, and then me, then Dill took a solo. He started playing and slowly everything became off. We all looked around at each other still playing.

Max stopped the song again, "have you played an improved solo before?"

Dill looked offended, "yes, I have."

Max put his hand on his chin in a confused pose. "I'm not sure why we are off then."

Bryan started speaking, "I wrote the song to be played in a twelve tonal technique."

Max shook his head, "that's right, Dill you have any experience playing this kind of music?"

Dill stood up straight, "Of course I do. Mr. Artez said I'm one of his best soloists"

"Well what do you solo on?"

"Whatever he gives me."

Max nodded, "See we play differently. You have to be a little more creative. Following the paper only takes you so far. We don't write down our solos and play it over and over again."

Dill's face had a slight red tone, "Mr. Artez said that kind of music isn't proper. You must have complete order and play everything as perfectly professional as you can. Playing outside of the paper makes everything rather barbaric."

Max sighed, "That's not completely true."

Dill gave him a strange expression, "why would you defend something barbaric?" Everyone in the room seemed like they were shot cold. We couldn't believe someone was accusing Max of liking something barbaric but at the same time; liking something barbaric couldn't be good. We would all be guilty of it. Max spoke normally, "I take Law classes, I know what is barbaric and what's not. The kind of music we play is ok and it's the kind only played at the Red Note." Dill didn't respond.

After we were done, Max started talking about the song one more time. "We have 5 minutes to perform. If the crowd likes us, then we may be there until the place closes as long as they are cheering our name. Now we can only have three solos, any more would be cutting into our time on stage."

Nick spoke up, "what do you mean?"

Max smiled, "We'll see if the crowd doesn't love us and if they don't cheers us on; then we are average at the Red Note. If we are average they might use us as a filler band between their main bands and as background noise. If they don't like us we may never come back. We only have 5 minutes. If we go over our time and the crowd isn't into it then the owners might get mad. So you three are soloing, only 40 seconds at most." He pointed to Jesse, Bryan and I. Dill wasn't happy. "Alright let's get our stuff and pack up the drum set."

Dill made his way to the door. Max looked around at our equipment, "you're not helping?"

Dill didn't look back, "I'll meet you there." he closed the door behind him with his guitar in his hand.

"Why is he with us?"

Max turned to Nick, "well the rules of the Red Note say all new bands must have 6 members minimum. Most people who play have around 15."

"Well he just made fun of my song. He shouldn't be part of us."

Max sighed, "Look we need him now. The song we have is great and better than most songs people hear nowadays. It's even better then songs performed at our campus concerts; maybe even better than some played at the Red Note."

Bryan jumped in, "What if he messes up? We have one shot."

Max was silent for a moment, "well we can't go without him. I mean the only reason I suggested we pick him is because he is one of the best in Mr. Artez's class."

Nick was upset, "but that's Mr. Artez's class. Anyone could be good if you memorize exactly what he tells you. His entire test feels like a memory game."

Max put up his hand, "we can't do anything about it now." he lowered his hand and pointed at the drums. "Let's get the drums packed. Later if we get the job we will replace him." Jesse started turning bolts on the drums; everyone came to help. The drums rested on a platform, the top was rubber with a wooden base. Bryan and Max lifted the platform while Jesse pulled out wheels from under it.

Everyone took the stands and symbols down and placed them in specific area to act like railings around the drum. They then hooked the toms to the rails. We then put the amps on the platform and closed them in with the railings. I picked up my guitar and put it in the case. Bryan fit his piano and chair on the platform then helped Jesse push everything. The rest of us carried whatever else we needed.

Max was the last to leave the room and locked the door. We all moved out of the way so Max could lead the way to the exit. Max went around a corner while Jesse and Bryan pushed everything behind Nick and me. A man stopped Max; I turned quickly to tell everyone else to stop so we wouldn't run anyone over.

The Man had a blue vest that said 'storage manager' running down one side. He was looking over Max's shoulder, "what's going on?"

Max started explaining, "We are moving some stuff out of storage." The man gave him a suspicious look then walked out of the way. We continued out of the building and waited on the street. Max sat down in front of the platform; Nick and Bryan were behind the platform. Jesse and I sat next to Max.

"Why are we sitting here? Shouldn't we be going now?"

Max turned to me, "well we are waiting for a pickup truck. I have a friend from transportation studies coming to help us for free."

Jesse started talking, "so does the law change when we leave this place?"

Max chuckled, "I'm not sure. There are so many rules, each rule with ten others to explain how the rule works. A lot of things can change; I still haven't finished all my studies."

"What Jobs do we get when we leave?"

Max turned to me, "Well, in sophomore year you will officially be put into class that will deal with your future job."

Jesse got his attention, "how do they determine that?"

Max smiled, "well it's a process that involves different factors. Soon you guys will have to take your blood examination. They will check your DNA to see what you're genetically like. They watch your grades in every class to see what you might qualify for; then they monitor your extracurricular activities. You take an extensive personality test. It's all put into a computer, some numbers and statistics are done and there you go."

"Do we have a say in any of it?"

Max turned to me again, "well the personality test-" he paused and got up heading to the back of the platform. "What are you guys doing?" Jesse and I ran around to see what was going on. Bryan and Nick were fighting over a bag on the ground. Max grabbed the bag from them, "are you guys stupid? We are on the streets! We are about to go perform, you can't be hallucinating while on stage." Max rolled up the bag into a small ball and put it in his pocket, "it's going to be hard to get rid of this."

Bryan went into a verbal rage, "we did this before! We haven't been effected before, none of the side effects that the health guy said is happening to us!" everyone was in shock. Bryan was angrily glaring at Max. He then looked around and saw everyone else with their mouths open. Bryan's face went from anger to sorrow. Max stood with a surprised expression. The first time any of us spoke back to him. Bryan seemed like he was about to tear up on the inside, "sorry, it was just expensive."

Max bent down and placed his hand on Bryan's shoulder, "how much did you pay?"

Bryan thought for a moment, "50 drops maybe."

Max stood up, "50 drops is a lot of money. Who sold it to you?" (The truck Max was waiting for pulled up). A man popped his head out the window and called out for Max. Max turned and started pulling the platform. Bryan quickly stood and said; "Jones Mill sold me it." he started pushing the platform.

"Well what are you going to do now?"

The back of the truck turned into a ramp. Bryan was pushing the platform up the ramp. He spoke disappointed by himself, "I won't see him again, I promise I won't pay that much again." we all sat around the platform on benches built into the sides of the frames. The ramp closed, Max went up front and the truck jolted. After a moment we all got used to the drivers lead foot and repeatedly stopping sharply. The driver could have been pulled over at any point for reckless driving if anyone reported him.

I tapped Jesse's knee then quickly started playing some simple poly-rhymes with my legs and hands. Jesse looked at me, he shook his head. I started playing louder and used my feet. Nick looked at me funny; I gave him a look to join in. Nick added to the rhythm and it went perfectly with mine. Bryan looked over and joined in right away. I nudged Jesse with my elbow to join. He chuckled to himself then joined with a brilliant pattern. We kept changing the rhythms and played off each other until the truck came to its last stop.

The ramp opened, Max came around back and started pulling the platform; Bryan went to help. As we came off, Max smiled at us, "You guys really love music. We hear you guys up front, you even made the car shake."

Jesse went around the platform, "Was it our music that shook the car or the driving?"

Everyone chuckled, "True but my friend was giving me compliments about you guys. This is a good way to start off the night."

The front of the building was packed with a line stretching across the building. Max told us to wait a while over by the door and waved at his friend in the truck. Max exchanged some words with the bouncer at the front door. The bouncer seemed angry over something. Max walked back and signaled down the street, "come on, we have to go around the building then head to a store quickly. Hurry up we don't have much time."

As we went around the street corner, Dill was strolling up the street in our direction with his guitar. Max waved; Dill looked at him, confused at first, and then waved back. We met up with him and Max started telling him what we were doing. "We have to enter through that side path there. Then we need to go to the store quickly." Dill knotted as if he was in the army; his eyes were red and glossy. He seemed like he didn't have a sense of direction.

We went into the side path with the platform. There were two garage doors on the back of the Red Note. Two men waited outside; Max walked up to them, "we are supposed to be playing in 30 minutes."

The men looked at us. One shook his head and spoke, "if you guys are playing you can't go on wearing that stuff." The other man walked around us, "you have to wear a standard suit from the dress code to perform; either all red, a shade of red or black for a dress up shirt. Tie is optional in any colors and then either black or red for the rest of the suit"

Max nodded, "we are just dropping off our equipment."

The man walked back to the door and helped the other man open one of the doors. We pushed the platform into a sketchy looking storage room. The men told us just to leave our equipment in the middle of the room and closed the garage door behind us. When Bryan and Max wheeled it into place, then Jesse hit some switches to lock the wheels.

Max waved and we all started hurrying out the door next to one of the garage doors. Dill was slowly strolling after us in a daze. We all followed Max down the street to a clothing store close by. As we came close to the door Max started giving us instructions, "just pick stuff that matches the dress code for now. Don't worry about the money; I'll pay for you guys. Just don't make me go bankrupt."

We all walked in and went straight to the suit and tie section. We ripped through sizes and hurried to the changing room like a commando operation. When we were ready we started plucking off the price tags we found by the cash register while Max paid. The cashier looked at Max, "will this be it?"

Max looked around, "where's Dill?" Max went over and found him slowly picking through clothes.

The rest of us were away from them waiting by the door. I turned to Jesse, "how much is this going to cost?"

Jesse made a face, "Right now, a lot. If we get the job, probably reasonable. If they love us, this would be pocket change."

Max walked over and started talking to the cashier, "how much for everything?"

The cashier stood up from the chair and put down a book. "You all late to an award ceremony or something"

Max shook his head, "in a way." The cashier looked at us all and started counting up the total on a machine. Max added, "We have one more by the way."

The cashier nodded, "right now that would be 500 drops." Jesse chuckled and we all turned to see Dill walking over. He had on an expensive suit that looked extra fancy, even more than the rest of us. Dill even grabbed an over coat to go with it. The rest of us didn't want to burden Max with getting us one so we all didn't even think about it. The cashier looked at Dill and turned his head, "um well that will be 750."

Max turned to us, "how much time do we have?"

Jesse answered quickly, "about 10 minutes we should be performing."

Max sighed, "Alright, let's get going." he managed to pay everything up front. We all started to rush out of the store; Dill tried to stroll along but Bryan and Nick rushed him. Everyone went back behind the Red Note and seen the men from last time. One guy smiled, "now you all look ready; especially him." he pointed at Dill. We went back into the door on the side.

A junior with a silk suit walked in and saw us around the platform. "Who's in charge here?" Max walked over, "what's your name?"

"Max-"

The junior cut him off, "we have been looking for you guys, and you're on in two minutes." Everyone quickly started rolling the platform. He started getting angry, "no you guys don't need any of that. Just take your guitars and bass. We have a drum set on stage and amplifiers, you can just tune a channel and play."

Bryan quickly called out, "what about a piano?"

The man sighed with anger, "we will pull one up." we took the guitars out of the cases and followed the man to the stage. He told us to wait behind the curtains. On stage was a swing band playing with 30 people on some stands.

A sound tech guy came over to us and started talking to us about the logistical stuff; the channels for the amplifiers, where the piano would be and so on. The band stopped playing and the audience started clapping as they walked off the other side of the stage. As they left the risers went down to form the floor of the stage. The sound tech told us to go out on stage and started pushing us. A microphone came out near the front of the stage on a stand. Over on the left side of the stage a piano was rising from under the stage. The drums were already centered on the back of the stage. The lights were so strong you could barely see passed the first row of tables from the stage; even then you had to squint to see the faces of the people sitting at the table.

We were all in place, by now everyone stopped cheering. It seemed like everyone was eating talking and not even caring that we were up here. The lights lowered a bit and I could see several people sitting on a balcony. They were our judges, and from what I could tell they didn't look impressed. They were the ones that rated how good they thought we did compare to how the crowd acted like we did.

Max turned to us and we all locked eyes. Max snapped his fingers, and then Jesse started up with a drum roll. Jesse played relaxed and at ease everything felt natural for us playing here. We started playing just like how we practiced and the crowd started noticing us. Max held the microphone in his hand and at the right moment started letting out his soul. The crowd seemed to stop whatever they were doing just so they could hear us. At this rate, if we didn't mess up, we had the job.

It came down to the solos. Max walked off to the side so everyone could see the soloist. Bryan went first, his fingers gracefully moved over the keys of the piano. He played it so well you wouldn't have noticed he messed up a couple times.

Max was watching the crowd and they liked us. I seen Max look up at the Judges and it seemed like they were taking notes down whenever Bryan made a mistake. You could only tell if you were analyzing the music instead of listening to it.

Max came back to the microphone early and Bryan ended his solo. This wasn't planned but we started going along with Max. The crowd was starting to cheer us on one at a time. The sound techs started playing with the lights and working hard to make us look even better; of course the only reason why they helped us was because the crowd comes first. Max stopped and looked over at me. I took a step forward and was about to start. Dill leaped forward on the stage and took the solo. He was spinning and swaying back and forth looking loopy; but the crowd seemed to like it and cheered us on more. The sound tech put a spotlight on Dill trying to make us look good. Dill slowed down and went from the song we were playing for a solo then somehow turned the song into one everyone from school knew and loved. He played the melody the singer would normally do and the crowd loved it. They started singing the words along with him. Luckily we knew the song and tried to improve and help Dill out by changing the song with him so it would sound good. How did we pulled it off, I don't know, it just happened.

We had a minute and a half left, Max signaled Dill to stop. Dill reluctantly ended his solo almost out of his will. Jesse started to do a drum roll and went into an amazing solo. Everyone started cheering and the crowd went crazy. It was as if Jesse stole the show. Max went up to the microphone as Jesse started finishing his solo. As soon as Jesse hit his last symbol Max started singing the chorus and we all jumped along with him. We finished the song going over our time limit by five seconds.

I looked up and seen the judges all-looking down taking notes as the lights dimmed into darkness. Everyone was cheering us on in the dark even though we didn't introduce ourselves with a name. Max started rushing us off stage before the lights went back on. We went behind the curtains on the other side of the stage. We then went to an open area and formed a circle, celebrating a job well done.

Max was off to the side watching us and thinking. Dill went over to Max and started arguing, "Why did you rush us off stage? They wanted another song!" Dill stood there in rage. Everyone went over ready to defend Max if anything happened.

Max calmly spoke, "If we don't play another song tonight, they are going to have a hunger to hear us again. They might even request us. Plus now every other group won't get the same reaction, leaving us with a good impression." Dill was angry but didn't have a reason to take it out on Max.

A sound tech guy walked over, "You have to leave, we need this area."

Max talked to the guy, "We left some supplies in the storage room."

"Come with me I'll show you how to get there." The sound tech guy took us through a hallway behind the stage to the storage room. He pointed to the door, "Grab what you need quickly. Leave through that back door." The sound tech guy went away.

Bryan turned to Max, "Where is the platform?" everything we put in the room was gone.

Nick walked in the middle of the room, "Do you think someone stole it all?"

Jesse went over to him, "They probably just moved it out if the way.

Bryan nudged Max's arm, "Let's go see what they did with it."

Max looked around, no one was here, Dill was gone. He told us to come close, "The instruments were never registered so technically we shouldn't have them. They probably found out about that and got rid of them so they wouldn't be suspected of breaking the law. It looks like we got the job anyway so getting all the stuff replaced will be easy and this time legal."

Jesse didn't seem to care that his drums were gone, he just stayed quite. We all walked out of the back door and saw the same two men standing in back of the Red Note. One of them called us, "you guys did well, can't wait to see you perform again."

Max waved and continued around the corner and down the street. Max turned to us, "See you guys did good."

Nick quickly jumped in, "You did good too." Everyone agreed.

Max smiled, "It's your skill they loved; you guys make me sound good."

Bryan was in front of us, "you're the reason why we are good, you taught us everything we know."

"Yea, I guess. Where do you guys want to eat for dinner?"

Nick was the first one to answer, "we should go to that place next to the English building. They usually have good cooks around."

Jesse thoughtfully said, "The place next to the library has senior chefs." Everyone thought about it and we decided to go there instead. We walked into the building and stormed a back table. Nick and I still had our instruments with us. A waiter walked over and asked us what drinks we wanted then went off.

Bryan was next to Nick and they both chuckled to themselves. I called them from across the table, "what's so funny?"

Bryan smiled and leaned over as if it was a secret, "Remember that girl from the gym we were talking to?"

"The one drawing our blood?"

"Yea, she actually showed up. I saw her off to the side with some friends."

"And so what?"

Bryan looked at Nick, "Well she was impressed with me."

Nick turned, "No she was impressed with me."

I stopped them, "how do you even know she was impressed with either of you?"

Bryan puffed up his posture, "I keep looking over and she kept catching my eyes like-"

Nick cut him off, "No she was looking over at me during your solo and I made her smile with my facial gestures." Now I knew why they messed up a couple times.

Bryan put his hand on the table and turned half his body to Nick, "No, see during my solo I gave her the eyes and she was smiling. I really made a good impression on her."

They started going back and forth. Max turned from his conversation with Jesse, "Guys, she was with her partner and she told me that she found it humorous when you guys were fighting over her earlier today."

Max fascinated Bryan, "You know her?"

"I see her almost every time I head to law class."

Nick seemed almost heartbroken, "She has someone already? She seemed like she enjoyed talking to us and even flirted with us."

Bryan smiled, "At least with me."

Max chuckled, "guys you all are going to get your lifetime partners at the end of the school year. Relax."

Bryan confessed, "Lifetime? I'm not ready for that. I'm still trying to find out what girls like."

Jesse tapped Max, "Do we have a choice in the matter?"

"Well, I mean the color we can choose you should know about your options." The guys laughed, Max didn't see what was funny.

Jesse was on not entertained by the joke, "Not the drum set, I meant about our partners?"

"O, all I can say is make sure your blood is clean, clear and on your pre-citizens test be as honest as you can. Other than that, you don't have a say in the matter."

"What's a pre-citizens test?"

Max turned to me, "It's probably the most important test you will ever take. You only take it once and people usually don't talk about it much after it's over because people don't question it or think it's a big deal."

Jesse listened closely, "how do you get a good grade on it?"

"Well it doesn't count for a grade. You won't be penalized for it; unless it's troubling. They don't tell you about how much it really affects your life until after you are dropped into law class and have to learn it. You guys will be told about it and you'll take it a week after I graduate. The next seniors after my generation will grade it. Since normally the difference generations don't mingle a lot here you probably won't know your graders. All they see is your answers and an ID number for the test that only you and the school know and uses to link you to the test. Of course the test in scanned by the computer but the computer gives a overall result that the grader has to interpret; then another grader comes and reinterprets it to insure they got it right without seeing the others interpretation. I had to do it last year and it wasn't fun."

The waiter came back with drinks, "What will you like to eat this evening?" everyone said what they wanted and the waiter walked off.

Nick tapped Max's arm, "You were saying? About the test?"

"Where was I?"

Bryan guided him, "you said we won't know the graders and how it's an important test."

Max re-gathered his thoughts, "Ok well you will be assigned a day and a room to report to. They will be strict about it and you are going to be stuck alone in a room for a while. Just follow everything they say. You will take 3 parts; first is the one you want to watch out for. Its nicked named the moral test. It evaluates you as a citizen. Do it first because they have specific questions that test you to see if you have any morality problems that resembles a barbarian. They use this to see if you believe what is correct and if you would act like a good citizen under situations you have to circle what you would do. If you fall outside the normal responses too much they will keep an eye on you."

Jesse stopped him, "is this legal?"

Max nodded, "Yes it is. They can monitor you under any conditions so long as they have reasons to believe you are a problem to public safety. Of course barbarianism is a problem and if you think outside what everyone else thinks you are a barbarian. The Law is written vaguely and the reasons are on general terms. The only thing that is clear is how they list out the ways they can track you; and it's a list let me say. O and if your answers aren't consistent or it doesn't match your normal record of conduct over the years to come, it won't be a good thing for you."

Nick seemed confused, "Since when do we have a record of conduct?"

"You guys already have something on for the incident earlier today with the illegal plants."

Bryan seemed nervous, "Will that affect us now?"

"Not too much; unless you are mixed in with other messes like this. They will keep this in the back of your records. If you keep getting in trouble they will eventually narrow things down and if your name pops up too much they will suspect you."

Jesse asked, "Can we clear it?"

The waiter came back with our food, "Stay clean for the next few years and people forget even the worst situations as long as they don't have to remember it or keep it in a file." The waiter went away.

I took a bite out of my sandwich then turned to Max, "what's the rest of the test about?"

Max gave a surprising answer, "You; the second part is the personal assessment test. It's basically a large booklet that asks you questions about what you like and your interest. It goes into details about what you like to do, what classes you liked, what kind of people you like to be around. What hobbies you have. This one determines what classes you will be put in for next 3 year and in part who your partner will be."

Jesse rubbed his chin, "and that's all they need to determine your life?"

"Well the blood test is supposed to help confirm parts of the written test."

Nick chuckled, "Don't we have those all the time?"

"Yes but this one is different. They use it to search your genes. I guess your genes can tell everything about you. I don't know the process or why it's that way but the science is supposed to support it somehow"

Bryan seemed skeptical, "So what you're saying is our genes could replace us telling you about ourselves?"

Max knotted, "I guess you need the biological test and a mental one to see if they line up."

Jesse started talking, "your genes are supposed to help influence what you are interested in; what your taste buds are like, how your brain learns, stuff like that. It's just a wonder on how far that can stretch too."

Nick was curious, "How does that help you with who you like?"

Max looked at Jesse, "Well I was talking with a biology teacher and he gave me a long rambling explanation. But, it went something like this; your genes make up your immune system and your body gives off chemicals signals to others and that lets a potential mate. Then we choose a mate based on factors like how different our immune systems are and other signals go off like how healthy our offspring could turn out. It was a longer explanation. Sometimes the science teachers forget you don't take their class."

Nick didn't seem happy, "That can't be it, there has to be more than that, right?"

Max turned to Nick, "Well I guess it takes into account what your interests are, your genes help make up the way you think or something so. I mean I guess they try to put you with someone you have the same interest as and someone you think you would like. I can't tell you how well it works really."

Bryan tapped Max's hand, "Then they really got you and Mary right."

Nick blurted out, "Who's Mary?"

We were all silent, "Mary is my partner." Max spoke with a calm expression.

"Why haven't you ever told us about her? Or why don't we see you with her."

Max replayed bluntly, "Because she's off with other guys." Everyone awkwardly started eating.

Bryan glanced at Nick condemning him for the awkward moment. Jesse tapped Max. Max looked over, "Yea?"

"So if we aren't happy with the results of the test can we get it changed?"

"Technically yes, realistically no. If you could I would have redone mine. I'm with her because I put answers down that I thought I wanted in a *'women'*. Unfortunately, we don't always think about what we want, we just want it. She told me she faked her answers because she thought they wanted the 'right answers.' Someone honest, sweet, sensitive, kind caring… turns out she wants the opposite of me. Everyone was looking away from Max. He continued, "If you want to retake the test you can; but if your results are too off from the last one… it gives a bad message. By Law everyone is required to take the test. By Law the test is graded and acted by standards required by law. In a way if the test is wrong, the Law is wrong. There are only two situations. Either we have to change the Law or the person faked and disobeyed the Law. By Law the Law is correct, so that leaves one more option."

"And this is how we run things?"

Max turned to me, "yes, this is our world and this is our life. The Law is the Law and the law governs us. The law is correct and perfect. The only thing that can be wrong is you."

Everyone finished their meals and the waiter left a bill. Max seemed gloomy like at practice. Lately it seemed as though he had a hanging cloud for a face. Max reached into his pocket and started pulling out some drops.

Jesse stopped him, "Let me help you." He started reaching in his pocket. Max didn't say anything. We all started reaching into our pockets and pulled out drops. We dumped our drops on the tables so max didn't have to pay; all the drops were in a pile over the bill. Max looked at the money, "you guys are short." He dropped 4 more drops into the pile.

Jesse tried going for the drops in his wallet, "I have extra".

Max stopped him, "No, I already paid just keep your money. We should be getting more soon." We all stood up from the table and went to our dorms.

I opened the door and Nick walked in behind me. Off to the left was his stuff and too the right was mine. On my side was a single bed close to the ground. His bed was up high like a bunk bed with his desk under his bed. In the middle on the wall from the door was a window with my desk under it. To the left next to Nicks bed was the door to the bathroom. Next to my bed was a closet. I walked in and placed my guitar next to my bed. Nick placed his bass next to his desk and started climbing up to his bed. I went over and sat at my desk.

Nick looked over at me, "what are you doing?"

"I need to redo my essay and make a second essay for tomorrow."

"How are you going to finish all that?"

"Well I'm just going to go through my notes and fill in the arguments Mr. Galvar said I should have used. I guess I will start on the second essay tonight and finish it in class tomorrow or something, maybe if I have free time. I don't have him until last period so I have time."

"What essay was it?"

"It was about barbaric ideas and arguments against them."

Nick jumped down, "Well I know Bryan is doing his now and Max had to have done one. Just ask one of them for the second essay."

"Didn't you hear Max? They are going to call that plagiarism."

Nick went through a small drawer under his bed. "People will only call it that if they find out; besides no one uses their own essay. It's too risky for your grade; if it's not *'perfect'*."

"How?"

"Well, look at your essay. If it isn't perfect then you aren't getting a good grade. Three grades under 90 means failing." He walked over to me with some clothes in his hand, "One thing I noticed is rewriting words is probably one of the only skills I learned so far." He walked into the bathroom. I turned and placed my hand on the desk. It started lighting up. I tapped an icon near the top and turned down the brightness. The shower in the bathroom went off. I started to pull up my essay and gathered my thoughts.

The next morning Nick was shaking me to wake up. My eyes opened and our alarm clock was ringing. He didn't even start getting ready. "How late did you stay up?"

"Not sure, I fixed my first essay and started the second." I lifted myself from the bed and turned off the alarm.

Nick sat next to me, "that thing went off for 5 minutes until I realized you weren't getting up. I'm surprised you slept through that."

"Yea well you know you don't have to wait for me to turn it off."

"I know but that's why I let you get up and use the shower so I can have extra time to sleep while you turned off the alarm." Nick walked away.

The first class of the day was math. Jesse, Bryan and I all had this class together. Nick's schedule was different and never seemed to mix with mine often, only for a handful of times. Max said, the only difference in freshman classes' was the teachers. From sophomore year and up we would take special classes. Some classes were only for specific jobs like Law classes.

Our math teacher had us take a test several days ago and felt it wasn't important for us to know our grades until the end of the week. Even if he finished grading over the weekend he wouldn't give them to us until next Friday. He sat at his desk with a large bread; his face was large and droopy. As he talked to us he was clean in his manner and he felt like he was better then everyone around him.

The class was silently doing advanced trigonometry. He was looking through the test and when he finished, he stood. "Luckily for all of you the school has an extensive grading system where each test has 1000 points. I have to grade according to the grading system; correct numbers, units, and calculations out to correct decimal places appropriate for the question, proper methods used for questions, work shown, and work done correctly, sentences written when appropriate, neatness of writing, organization... as you can see all of this helps maximize your scoring and seeing your performance. If it were up to me, I would simply give you a problem; if your answer is correct with proper units you get credit, if you get one thing wrong you get no credit. Many of you would have lower scores simply because of units and making your answers not clear enough so I can glance at your answers and grade it."

The man walked around and handed the tests to everyone started with the highest grades. "Here you are, you will have a bright future." He walked over in my direction and stopped at Jesse, "brilliant, you are a star student." He went around the room. After a few visits the words went from 'great students' to 'you can make it in this world' to your below average, pick it up before you fail life.' He came to me second to last, "you have an 8 percent error. You're below average. At this rate you have no future." He threw the test on my desk disgusted. I picked up the test and looked at what I did wrong. The only real mistakes were a handful of signs, errors, and some decimal errors. It would have only come to 4 percent error but he did not like my organization and took off points.

The room was gloomy while the man went back to his desk. He went over the test without looking at the class and not caring about questions. He only looked up to tell people to stop sleeping. How he seen people sleeping is kind of a mystery because he never looked up from his desk unless he had to.

Later at lunch we all decided to eat something fast so we can find Max. Luckily we only have blood drawing on Monday and Thursdays so we had plenty of time to roam the campus looking for him. He was at some kind of event being held outside the history building. The law classes were part of the history building simply because there was no other place to put it. Around the side of the building was a courtyard where the law class took over for a debate. By the wall of the building was a podium with two tables on the sides of the podium. Max was sitting at one table with two other people. In front of them were rows of chairs, most of them empty with a handful of Law teachers and two sophomore students in Law. There were about 30 chairs but only 10 were being used. We stood at the edge of the courtyard listening for Max.

Jesse and I tried following the debate. Turns out, the debate was over a new controversial topic that could be argued either way. The existing topic was 'should technological discoveries be utilized as soon as they are found or should we wait.' The first guy that spoke was boring and was defending the statement that we should wait. The guy had very poor examples and seemed like he wasn't interested in the topic.

Now it was Max's turn. He had on the suit that he used from the performance at the Red Note. Max took the podium confidently reading from a paper, "How can we wait for progress. The moment we stop pushing forward is the moment we push nowhere. If we are afraid to embrace new ideas then we are afraid to keep our nation for greatness. How else could we embrace the rejection of barbarianism if we aren't open to ideas that might work? The idea of free speech is an idea easily excepted, but that knowledge is dangerous. This can be hard to see." Max looked up and seen us all sitting in the back row. He seemed startled for a moment. He looked at the podium, "How else can we make progress in our industry or how can we finish the new space probes or accomplish the idea of colonizing the cosmos."

Max had a way of capturing people's attention. After he spoke they took a brake and planned on getting back to their riveting debate next class session. Everyone, even the teachers, went up to Max and congratulated him on his speech. He excused himself and went over to us. He told us to follow him and we all went to a place to eat.

"Max, your speech was the best one there."

Max turned to Nick, "It was ok."

Jesse spoke, "you really study your material"

Max shook his head and held the door open for us as we went into a coffee shop. He had us sit in one of the back corners. A waiter came over and took Max's order. We said we didn't want anything and the waiter went off. Max didn't seem happy and it didn't seem like any of us knew why. Bryan finally asked if Max was ok and he started to confess.

"Not everything I said was fully me."

Everyone was surprised, "Do you mean you were assigned what argument you had to defend?"

Max looked at me, "No, I picked my side. See, I found out the reason they have these debates is to see who has conformed their ideas to the law. Those who stick to the Law are given higher positions and those who don't are pushed aside given more meaningless un-influential jobs. I picked my side because we already have Laws about how to deal with scientific findings. If the science governing organizations say it's approved then it is. If not, you don't hear about it. They clump scientific ideas into categories and if it happens to fall under a category they simply say if they are important or not by the category. A lot of times findings in astronomy aren't important so they just don't tell the general public. We don't have the ability to travel to the stars so until we do and someone has a realistic plan we don't talk about space. See if an asteroid was going to collide with the earth, no one would hear about it because we can't do anything about it and frankly the law keeps us safe from anything. If the law can't protect us from an asteroid then we simply don't talk about it. If we find a product for food consumption and if it doesn't give you health benefits you thought it did, you wouldn't hear about it because the law already banned unhealthy foods. The law is perfect so there aren't any more unhealthy foods left, or so they say. A lot of these ideas are just not talked about. Personally I think everything should be tested and brought forth individually. I hate all these one size fit all rules that are so specific we need a hundred other one size fit all rules to cover what the first rule left out."

Max put his hands on his face. Everyone sat in confusion. Bryan tapped him, "are you disagreeing with your profession?"

Everyone was silent as the waiter awkwardly gave Max his plate while we sat there. The waiter went and Max spoke, "I don't know. I don't hate the profession; I hate what we have done with it."

Nick tried to be sympathetic, "Maybe you just need a break from the stress."

Max sighed, "No, I'm going to break it down for you guys. Every movement you make every action you try to do; it feels like there are five rules for each. Everything is so complicated. Just simply a can of soda is packaged and it takes several regulations all of which making things; more expensive to meet, hard to carry out and unnecessary. The fact that a can must be made of 1 millimeter of aluminum, 0.1 millimeters of leaf and 1 millimeter of drink protective material. The aluminum is regulated so your drink stays cold, keeps production cost down with cheap material, helps eliminate competition, plus there are regulation on the purity and composition of the aluminum structure and completely different set of rules on how to refrigerate the cans. The lead is mandatory so toxins from the Aluminum and UV rays from the sun don't mess with the contents of the drink. Now the purity of the lead and how it is melted, applied, solidified, and crafted into a shell with in the can depends on the drink it will hold. Then the protective material is so complicated; the material has to help preserve the drink, keep the lead out, and prevent any chemical changes between the material and the drink. It all varies between drink-to-drink. A single can of soda cost five drops more than it would be if they simply had paper containers or some other form of a container, plus the lead in the cans slowly add to the amount of fuel transportation needed to move the weight. But we can't use these because of health Laws written hundreds of years ago making this mandatory.

Scientific research for new containers is rejected because the Law has the 'perfect solution.'" Max sighed and went to eat.

Jesse decided to speak, "Well most of this doesn't affect us. What's wrong with all of this?"

Max stopped chewing and swallowed, "It's too much to have. A lot of the rules we have effect us and you guys don't even see it because of how accustom you are to them. See if you simply are a person in society and move along doing what everyone else does; you don't see them. When you move outside the lines, so much as a foot, if your thoughts go outside of the box or even touch the sides of the box; see that's when you see. You can't see outside of Law because you are stuck and limited by the Laws. You can't be alone for too long without signing in to some places. You can't go to some places just to be alone. Being anti-social is a problem because you aren't surrounded by other people to model your thinking. There are just so many things you guys haven't noticed because they have been around you for so long. The funny thing is the Law is supposed to keep us safe, give us opportunity and punish people who do evil; but really it turns us into criminals and keeps us from moving anywhere in life, just modeling us."

Bryan thought to himself then spoke almost as if he was defending the Law, "Well what about us working at the Red Note? We are getting places."

"Yes but that's only here, after this school it's different. See things like the Red Note and other stuff keeps us from thinking about life too much. We are so consumed with the social part of humans we don't look for others. This campus isn't like the rest of the world. We are actually cut off from the world. See here we are trained to think like the world so when we join the world we hit like a puzzle. It's actually easy to get away with stuff at this school because the school runs slightly different then the world from what we were told. If they knew we had unregistered instruments we wouldn't be where we are."

Nick spoke innocently, "why?"

"Because when I told you where to get the instruments from, I knew what I was doing. When we were sold the instruments, the previous owners reported they threw them out otherwise they would still have ownership of them. You can't own instruments until you are a sophomore and you have to be in music classes. You can only borrow them for a time, which is what I told you guys to do; but that's a hassle and we needed paramount instruments so we didn't have to return them after so many hours. If we are found with our, instruments, even though we bought them, to the system and to our Law, we stole them. Every non-edible object is registered until it is reported throughout when you turn it into waste management. Even something like a pen is registered to you, when you buy it from a cashier. Who cares right? But if that person wants the pen back, you are on the wrong side of the Law if authorities look for you. Think about this, those suits you guys own are legally mine. What if someone bought you something and wanted it back? You are in trouble if you took it from them even if it was a gift. That's why we are told not to share personal belonging and they just say it's for health reason and your spreading bacteria."

Jesse and I were the only two who could follow Max and see what the problem was; Bryan and Nick were looking at each other as if they didn't see the problem or maybe they didn't want to see it. Max ate while everyone was awkwardly looking at each other. Max was facing his food and eventually broke the silence; "I got a message from the Red Note."

Bryan pushed the mood forward, "what was it?"

Max still staring at his food with a gloomy look, "We got the Job, tomorrow is the first day. Three hundred drops per night we play."

Jesse spoke thoughtfully, "How many nights do we play?"

Max looked up from his food, "Well we have a special set up. The guy that passed on the message explained how the Red Note works. There are four ranks of entertainers. Because of our performance we are bumped up to rank two. If more people knew us we would be rank three." Bryan and Nick leaned back with pride while Max continued, "See normally we have to play five nights a week for up to three hours as a filler band in-between the important bands. At rank two, we have more flexibility and just have to play a minimum of eight hours a week. We can choose any time slots that are open. The lower ranked filler bands have to wait for us to pick what we want for hours. The more hours we get the less low ranked bands can work. The more we play the more we are known. If our performances are as good as yesterdays, we will rank up."

I interrupted him, "What if we go up in ranks?"

"The guy just told me we have to play no more than two hours a week but with 500 drops each hour. He didn't tell me anything more than that."

Bryan questions him, "Why do we have to play less?"

Jesse answered, "at that point it's more special when we play so people pay more."

Bryan seemed to be so surprised at this genius. Jesse turned to Max, "What are our benefits?"

Max finished his food, "We have to share the practice rooms with rank one bands. We don't have to bring a drum set. Piano, microphones, and amplifiers will be there. They will provide us with that stuff. We don't have to set up or pack up stuff, only rank one bands do. We just have to bring our guitars and if we leave them, the sound tech will grab them for us. We have locks that can fit some guitars and a couple suits at once. We still have to use the standard dress code. We can get into the Red Note for free and bring someone at half price. If we hit rank three, guest are free. O yes and for the practice rooms; they only have four but we get priority over the rank one bands. So if there is an empty room we get it before the lower ranks can use it, even if they are next to go on."

Another waiter walked over and picked up Max's plate. The waiter glanced at him then at all of us, "Hey didn't you guys play at the Red Note yesterday?" We all shook our heads. The waiter smiled, "I seen you guys, you really know your stuff." The waiter looked around at our faces, "I see you dropped the guitarist. That's good, if it weren't for the fact that yesterday was so cheap to get in, the less intelligent class-men wouldn't have been there to cheer him on. Most people who go to the Red Note aren't into that cheesy pop music he tried to play; but you all pulled it off fairly well." The waiter walked off.

Nick spoke bluntly, "What are we doing with Dill?"

Max waved his hand so he could get out of the seat, "I'll talk to someone at the Red Note. Either we have to drop him today or we have to find someone and replace him when we can. I'm not sure if they will let us go on with one man down."

We all headed out the door. Bryan tapped Max before he could leave, "Are we practicing today?"

Max let out a sigh, "I can't."

Nick went in front of him, "Why not?"

Max had his usual gloomy tired face; "I have to spend my recommended four hours a week with Mary."

Nick was confused, "You have to spend recommended time?"

Max nodded, "Yes, the Law recommends it, it's a problem if you don't listen to the Law. We put it off for a while now. If we don't spend time today it will look bad."

Jesse spoke, "Can they tell if you don't?"

Max shrugged, "Not sure, if anything, Mary could just say we haven't and I would get in trouble."

Nick spoke in an annoyed confused voice, "Why would she do that?"

"Money, my stuff. It's the only way to be single again. Either your partner dies or they are a criminal and are removed. There aren't plans in place to be remaindered ironically because the law would seem flawed if it would pick your second perfect match. But still they don't account for human error and how we make mistakes. You could be happy with your partner for life but sometimes people aren't looking for a partnership. In my case it gets you in a tight spot." Max walked off.

Nick turned to us, "Why would she want to be single?"

Bryan answered, "So she can 'mingle' with anyone she wants without being judged." We all went off to different classes.

I handed my make-up essays to, Mr. Galvar, to the class they were due. Mr. Galvar took my essays and said nothing about them. He almost seemed confused as to why I was handing him two essays. More than likely he won't grade them because he'll probably forget. We normally don't do extra credit, if we fail we fail, few teachers really care to put in the extra work to add extra credit to your grade.

After class I was in my room playing my guitar. Bryan and Nick walked into the room. "Hey come on, we are heading out."

I stopped playing and looked up at them, "Where are we going?"

Nick walked over to me; "We are going to spy on Max and Mary."

"So you guys want to stalk him on his date?"

Bryan sighed, "No, we aren't stalking or spying on them. We are going to see how their relationship really is."

I Looked around, "Where is Jesse?"

Bryan spoke, "We told him. He wasn't interested and said he had something to go to."

"What does he have to do?"

Nick walked over by the door, "Not sure, he just walked off and didn't tell us."

Bryan stood in the doorway, "Are you coming?" I shrugged and put my guitar away.

As we walked down the street Nick and Bryan were talking while I was right behind them. "Do you guys even know where he is supposed to be?"

Bryan turned to me, "I remember him talking about how he was going to take her to the fields to watch a game then go to dinner."

Nick chuckled, "I don't think that's where Max would take a girl on a date."

Bryan turned to him, "It was my idea. He was going to take her to the movie then to a nice restaurant; but I changed his mind. No point on taking her when he's going to have to pay for everything and she wouldn't care. If a games going on, then it would be cheaper than a movie."

Nick seemed perplexed, "Well when you put it that way. I was expecting him to just take her and sit under a tree while he reads a book."

Bryan shook his head, "That's not him."

Nick replied, "That's what he would do with us."

"That's because when he hangs out with us, he has a lot on his mind; and even still he's always helping us with stuff. When you're with a girl that is supposed to have your attention, it's different."

I interrupted them, "So why are we going to bug him again?"

Bryan answered, "We aren't going to speak with him; we won't try to let him see us. We are just going to see how she is so we know what not to answer on that test he told us about."

We found Max sitting in some stands watching a football game. Max was on the top row with Mary. Mary was standing and cheering; following the crowd. Max was just sitting reading a book blocking out everything. If you didn't know they were partners you would have never known the reason Max was even there. He wasn't paying attention to the game and was really just taking up a seat. Luckily this wasn't a real game and no one had to pay for seats. You still had to get tickets because of the Law regarding how many people could safely sit in the stands at any given moment; or at least that's what I think Max would say.

We were on the ground standing off to the side of the stands. When the game was done everyone was cheering while Max simply closed his book and waited for Mary to leave. We tried waiting away from the exit just so we could see Mary and Max, but they wouldn't notice us. When Max and Mary finally left the stands, Mary had Max waiting for something. Mary didn't even look at Max or face his direction. The most they did was exchange a few words then sat in silence.

Bryan and Nick were trying to lip-read what they said and came up with something like; "Why are we waiting?"

"I'm waiting for a friend." They weren't positive if that's what was said until another girl walked over; the girl who did our blood drawing in gym. Mary grabbed Max's hand when she seen the girl and rushed over. Mary looked excited and was saying something. The girl had a smile and they exchanged words. Max stood there silently trying to smile and looked around.

Bryan and Nick tried to understand what they said. They understood something like; "Hey Mary, how was the game?"

"Great I got some news."

The girl said something they couldn't understand.

"Yes! We are moving up in life." Mary hugged Max, "he is so amazing."

"That's nice where are you going?"

Mary seemed to be bragging, "He's taking me out for dinner."

"O how nice, I'll let you get to It." the girl walked off. When she was gone, Mary let go of Max's hand and they walked off. Max silently walked behind her. We followed from a distance until Mary was stopped by a group of people. She smiled and grabbed Max close. The group had four guys and two girls.

Bryan and Nick were trying to figure out what they said but couldn't tell. The only thing they could understand was; Mary was bragging on Max. One of the guys started talking to Max while everyone else talked to Mary. Max and the guy were facing away from everyone.

Mary was mainly talking with the guys. She started walking over to the guys; she was locking eyes with all of them. She then started getting playful with the guys and after a handful of words she embraced the most appealing guy out of the group. The guy was wrapping his arms around her and they were cuddling. After a moment the group was leaving, Max was still talking with one of the guys. Mary quickly tried to slip a kiss with the guy around her. She turned to see Max watching her give his last words to the guy. They both walked on acting like nothing happen.

We followed them and they went into a small diner and sat by a window. We sat across the street just so we can see what was going on. Mary was distracting herself with anything she could; reading the menu five times over after ordering, trying to listen to music, giving guys looks even when they were with someone. She did everything but look at Max or even listen to him when he tried to talk to her. It looked like he was trying to have a casual conversation but she wasn't interested. Max smiled several times while talking to her; Mary spoke with the minimal amount of words possible. By the tine their food came, Max seemed to have given up, again. They ate and didn't even look at each other.

Mary pulled out a glass pad from her pocket. Something seemed to happen and they exchanged words. Mary then left with a smile. Bryan and Nick lip read, "Hey looks like our time is up I have to run somewhere."

"In a rush? Don't you want to finish?"

"Nope." Max was stuck with a bill for both plates, even though one barely had a bite out of it.

We decided to leave. Bryan went his way while Nick and I went back to our room. On the way back, Nick seemed deep in thought. "What's on your mind?"

He turned, "I'm not sure if I want a partner."

"Why? Because of Max?"

"Well I mean, can a simple paper and blood test really show who you should be with? I mean what if they have been getting everyone wrong all along?"

"Well if they did, only the people who have it wrong would know. If they complain or something, then the government would step in and someone would probably disappear."

"Well still it doesn't seem right. I mean it's like we learned everything there is to know in the virtual world, but I mean still this can be wrong. Even if it is science, nothing is even proven, so how can we know our genetics and whatever else we are in control of?"

I couldn't respond so we simply walked back to our room without another word. Later when we were both alone in the room; he leaned over the side of his bed, "I don't think I'm taking the test."

I looked up at him from my desk, "They are going to know. The most you can do, I guess, is go for what's best and try to keep it honest for everything other than your partner."

He looked confused, "why do you say that?"

"Because if you put what you want, you may not really know what you are getting or at least that's what I got out of our adventure."

"I know what I want."

"But do you know what that means? Look at Max."

"Well I mean not every girl is like that."

"True, but I mean come on you know deep down the girl you would want, especially before you seen Mary, is not the kind of girl you should be with. I mean just think about the traits you would pick and then think, will that only be with me?"

"I hate this it's like there is no way to win. There has to be a way to win. Something always wins in a situation. What about when I'm dead? Who wins then?

"Well if someone doesn't like you, then they win. If not then the birds and worms will win."

"Thanks."

"Well I guess what I'm saying is there is some way to win no matter what. You just have to try to find a way to be in the winning seat."

"Please I've been doing that and now we are at the Red Note. Unfortunately that means nothing because in the bigger picture I'm still losing."

"Well I guess it depends on what you define as a win; and what its worth in your life." Nick started staring into space at the ceiling, and then went to bed.

Saturday morning I slept in later than usual. It was around 11 am; Nick and Max were talking in the room. I picked my head up from the pillow. They were sitting in chairs by the door. Nick looked over, "He's up."

I rubbed my hands across my eyes, "What are you guys doing so early?"

Max spoke, "It's 11. I came to see how you guys are doing and to let you know what's going on."

I sat up, "we are playing at the Red Note right?"

Max nodded, "I talked with them and we can play with just the five of us for our first week."

Nick tapped his arm, "Why do we have to have an extra person?"

Max waved his hand as I finished getting ready, "It's to avoid any school money distribution problems. There's a set of Laws that apply only to the school money management that are supposed to model the rest of the world. But there are some rules that only apply here."

I was trying to catch up, "So what does that have to do with the Red Note?"

"We'll see money distribution is everything. Everything can't be paid equally but they can tax and mingle things to make everyone equal. We don't have to pay taxes until we leave but the stores do. They can find ways of keeping money if they have more employees. It gets complicated but the stores get to keep so much money in taxes if they have more employees and they don't regulate how much they are paid, just the minimum pay. Between this and some factors they used to calculate the tax owed, they can find ways of hiding money. In the Red Note's case, they have loads of money. I heard they have their own bank in the basement somewhere but I don't know how true that is."

Nick was surprised, "They must really know what they are doing."

Max nodded, "little knowledge can get you far. A couple generations ago, before I came, two partners decided to open the Red Note. I heard the guy was in Law class and his partner was in economics. I think they cheated the system together."

Nick chuckled, "you have so much faith in humanity."

Max smiled shortly, "I just know how people work. You're only yourself if you are the same when the Law is watching and when it isn't watching." We took a turn out to the streets and headed to the music building, "By the way Bryan and Jesse are waiting for us."

"What are they waiting for?"

Max turned to me, "We are going to try to replace Dill today and look for anyone to replace him."

"Won't he be mad if he walks by and sees us or something?"

Max shrugged, "He will find out eventually and I think he is playing in Lacrosse game today anyway."

Nick added, "If not this will be awkward for him."

On Saturdays everyone could walk around freely without classes. Most of the time people did one of two things; they simply hung around catching up with each other or they worked to get more money. A lot of the time people used whatever they learned in class on Saturdays; like the chiefs would cook all day, musician put on shows and those in management would keep stores open. A lot of the time big sport tournaments went on all day, botanist worked in the green house for fun. The thing that was especially good for us was, was the fact that any serious musicians was always at the music building on Saturday.

Jesse and Bryan were standing under a streetlight handing out fliers. We walked over, "How is it going?" Max waited for a response.

Jesse shrugged, "Well we got the fliers cheap from the printing department. We handed out five so far. Four people crumbled them and tossed it. One guy saw the name Red Note on it and talked to us."

Max spoke, "is he willing to join?"

Bryan shook his head, "he just saw that we were playing at the Red Note and congratulated us. Most people won't even take a flier."

Max walked passed them, "Come with me." Everyone followed without hesitation. We came to one of the outdoor stages where different bands were playing. Max told us to wait and he went over to talk to some sound tech guys by the stage. In front of the entrance to the stage were chairs set up with a couple of bands waiting to play. In front of the stage was a crowd of people and around the crowd were tents set up with different things going on. This was the usual set up for weekends as long as it didn't rain.

As we all waited for Max, we were examining the bands playing; the drummer, bassist, guitarist, singer. We went back and forth criticizing what they did wrong and admitting what they did right. Max came over to us, "We have five minutes after this band. Let's get ready."

"I thought we were going to try to get a new member?" Bryan was by Max's side.

"We are, play through the song once, two solos and then just play as background noise while I try to recruit someone."

Jesse spoke, "What are we doing for instruments?"

"The drum set stays, they have a piano for any band to use and we can borrow a guitar and microphone."

Nick smiled, "This feels too easy."

"Well there was a line of bands that were supposed to play. I used the Red Note card to try and talk our way in. As long as you guys do everything right we will be good." We all waited by the side of the stage waiting to go on. The band that was supposed to be next started arguing with the sound techs and glaring at us. When it was our turn the host of the event came up.

Normally the teacher and school staff ran things but on weekends the staff in charge discipline are the only ones around to monitor us. The rest of the adults went off to their own parts of the school grounds. During the weekends, we ran everything. The host was someone who took social media classes, which frankly they just learned how to predict what people liked for entertainment. We all came onto the stage while the guy was getting the crowd ready to hear a band from the Red Note. Some of the sound techs handed us our instruments and rolled out a piano. The host walked off when we were ready.

Max stepped up to the microphone. The crowd of people paying attention was small. Some people over at the tents looked over but many people didn't care. The drums started up with a solo. The piano jumped in with the notes starting in the higher range and sweeping down to the lower notes. Bryan then played a crisp 'A' flat major chord and we all started the song. Max sang and everyone instantly started paying attention. The crowd slowly started coming to the front of the stage. We took our solos and the crowd was happily bobbling along. When we were ready, Max walked forward while we played softly. "If anyone here is interested, we need one more person on our band. What instrument you play doesn't make a different. But we need one more talented individual."

It was something about the way he spoke. Max was just good at it. You could tell every Musician in the audience wanted to join. Even the band we cut in line seemed like they were now fighting about leaving their band. Max turned to us and smiled. We picked up the music and Max started singing to the end of the song.

I looked into the crowd and saw Dill far off behind the crowd. From his look I could tell he knew what was going on. He was staring down Max with a hard look. I'm not sure if anyone else noticed him. Everything was done; we had to exit through a back way. Dill disappeared.

We ended up going through the music building and outside away from the crowd out to the front of the building. Some of the musicians that were serious went to find us and crowded around the front. After a moment there was a line of people with instruments, all wanting to be accepted by us.

Max spoke loudly, "if you want to join you must have your instruments ready to play. We will not be here forever." Many people ran to get there; those who already had one didn't care that their band was up next. Max asked for a flier and a pen. He then turned to the first person in line. "What's your name?"

"Alley Farcum."

"Lets see what you got." Max sat on the ground and wrote down the name. Alley hesitated then played. After, Max looked up, "Alright, thank you." Alley walked off worried. Max then turned to us, "what do you thik? 1 to 5?" Max wrote down a 3 next to his name. We all wrote down our scores and then Max turned to the next person. This went on for two hours. We finally had to stop because they were shutting down the music building so they could get ready for evening concerts. It was probably a good thing this happened. Many of the people that were performing for us barely started getting a two or higher.

The line disappeared and we tried to walk away from another crowd. As we walked, Max was going through the names of everyone we seen; trying to ask us what we thought of each one. I felt bad because it seemed like Max was the only one paying attention. Max stopped and then tried to look for the highest scores he could find.

"Ok what about these circled ones?" We all huddled around Max looking at the back of some fliers with names and numbers.

A guy walked up to us. He was dressed like he just came out of a computer tech class. His hair was crazy and he had large glasses, his body was really thin. We all looked up; he had a smile and a clarinet. We all looked up at him, "hello? I'm here to try out. For your music group."

We all looked at each other. "Well I guess you can be the last person of the day." Max seemed like he only said this to be polite. The guy smiled, he had braces, it was very unusual to see anyone who actually needs braces; A lot of the people learning dentistry stuff love when that one rare person who needs any work on their mouth just so they can practice on them. He put the mouthpiece to his lips and blew a sharp note. The reed squeaked; he licked his lips while Bryan and Nick chuckled. The guy then started playing a song we all knew perfectly. It was a short song, only twelve bars long. He then played it again and again; each time changing the style of it making it sound like pop, then swing, then funk. Each time the song sounded more and more brilliant.

Bryan and Nick were stuck between having their Jaws dropped and laughing at how the guy danced while playing. By far he was both the goofiest and greatest talent we heard today. Max smiled, "What's your name?"

He stopped playing, "Timothy"

Bryan gave a look, "Do you have a nickname?"

"Tim, why?"

Max nodded, "Because you have the job." Tim smiled and jumped with excitement. Everyone looked at Max.

Nick chuckled, "Dill is going to be so mad…"

Max reached out to shake Tim's hand, "Go and get a suit that complies with the Red Notes dress code; meet us there at 5:30." Tim reached out and over excitedly shook Max's hand.

"I will be there early, you can count on me." Tim then ran off.

When he was far enough Bryan tapped Max, "Why did you let him in? Don't we all have to agree?"

Max smiled, "See, we need another person. He is a great musician. He even played better than everyone else."

Nick gave a puzzled look, "H`e's dorky…."

Max chuckled, "yes and that will set us apart from the other bands. He just needs to be cleaned up and get contacts. He will bring us what we need. People are going to love him for his personality."

Jesse spoke, "You really think so?"

Max nodded, "Everyone wants a laugh. They will laugh at him then with him and relate to him. His personality will show and then they will love him." Everyone didn't see what

Max was talking about except for Jesse. "Come on, let's start getting ready. We have to meet Tim at the Red Note in a couple hours. It would be nice to practice before we go on."

We all went to our rooms to get ready. While we were getting ready Nick called me in our room. "Max is crazy, Tim isn't what we need."

I was in the middle of buttoning my shirt, "Well I'm sure Max knows what he's doing."

Nick walked over with his vest undone and his collar messed up, "Tim is going to bring down our reputation. We can't have this, I mean you know it's true."

I looked over and sighed then continued buttoning my shirt. "I don't know if it was smart or not. All I know is, Max got us together from the beginning. He hasn't been wrong yet. The only person as smart if not smarter than him is Jesse; and Jesse seems to approve. We just need to trust Max. Worse comes to worse, we simply become an average band at the Red Note or get downgraded. We will still be set with money." I put on my vest then buttoned it. Nick didn't say a word; he simply finished getting ready and we walked over to the Red Note.

Max, Jesse and Bryan were waiting outside the Red Note. When we met them, Max told us we had to wait for Tim. Bryan and Nick looked at each other with disappointment. When Tim finally arrived he had on a suit, his hair was greased back and he had on a new pair of glasses with his clarinet on his hand. We then walked around to the back entrance of the Red Note.

Max already got a room for us to practice in. The room had a drum set in a cage, piano off to the side, a microphone in the center of the room, a guitar and bass along with head sets so we could all hear each other. We all got ready while Max talked to Tim, "So this is the music." he handed Tim some sheet music. "I know its short notice but just do what you can. Have you played this kind of music before?"

Tim looked through the song; "Yes, I have touched on some of this before."

"Good let's see what you got." Max turned to us, "one, two, one two three four."

We all started up right away. Tim was silent at first examining the songs. Max started singing and Tim jumped in with him. Tim somehow added something to the song. He gave it a sound that really completed everything and made it feel welcoming. He played as if we all played together for years.

We decided to play solos and Max had Tim go first. Tim played and it was flawless. We didn't think he could play that well on the spot. When our practice was done Max told us, "On the nights we play, we can go into the crowd before and after we perform for free; but if you want a meal or drink you will have to pay. If you want to go up there now, you can." Bryan and Nick headed for the door, "Just make sure you're behind the stage by 7 the latest."

It was just Max, Jesse, Tim and I left in the room. Max started a conversation with Tim, "so what grade are you in?"

"I' a junior"

"Two years left. The rest of these guys are freshman. When did you pick up your clarinet?"

Tim pushed his glasses up, "well I only wanted to work with computers; and well after I took the test, I guess they found some genes in me that showed I liked and would be good at clarinet. Sophomore year, the school put me in music classes for clarinet on the side with computers." Jesse and I looked at each other.

"That's a lucky break. Who did your test match you with?"

Tim had a large prideful smile, "Jill Rusma."

Max had a surprised look, "She's pretty."

Tim couldn't help but show off, "I know and I'm with her."

"I heard a lot of juniors were fighting over her before the test."

Tim shook his head, "Yes well, I guess I just have what's right. My genes are the best for her and that's how it is. Who's your partner?"

Max tried speaking without emotion, "Mary"

"Steres?"

"No, the other one." Tim was silent for a moment with a sorry look. Max broke the awkward silence, "So why do you like computers?"

Tim changed his face from sorrow to Joy, "I loved the virtual world we were in. I loved the world and creativity that went into making it. I want to do things like that."

Jesse spoke, "Well what about it? You want to redesign it?"

Tim seemed like he had a light bulb going on for years, "No see I have a revolutionary idea. See we spend all of our lives in this world and even with our perfect Law it still seems like we have a void on the inside." Max glanced at us, "see I have an idea; why not use those pods and use them for entertainment. Why not try to use them so we all could live in our own worlds. See I thought we could use the pods and the software to create a personal world for everyone. See a world we can control; One that we would love waking up every day and love visiting; one we can feel we belong too. One we had complete control over and we could manipulate whenever we wanted to."

Jesse spoke, "How do you think that will catch on?"

Tim seemed like he thought all of this out, "Easy, people pay so many drops a month to have their world running."

Max interrupted, "we have to go now. Grab the bass for Nick and the guitar." I went and grabbed both instruments.

We went behind the curtains and waited for the people on stage to end. Max looked around, Bryan and Nick weren't here yet. Max looked around the curtains being careful not to be seen. Bryan and Nick were at a table talking with some guy with long hair and a mustache. Max turned to Jesse, "Can you get them please?" Jesse nodded and went off. Jesse disappeared for a while. Max saw him talking to the guys. They all walked back just seconds before we had to go on. We all took the stage quickly and started up. Everyone loved us and the night went exactly as planned.

When we were done we all decided to eat at the Red Note. The six of us ordered our meals and Max paid for us all. "Are you sure you want to do this?" Tim wasn't comfortable with Max paying.

"Yes, we are getting paid today anyway. Don't worry about it."

"Well can I ask where you get the money for all of this? I thought you guys just started working for the Red Note. So I know you couldn't have made this much yet."

Max shrugged, "You know how we have the worldwide school stock market? Well I invested in it. Some school stores in the south are making a lot of money. I invested in them freshmen year and they have been growing since."

Nick jumped in, "I thought only people who worked in economics could do that?"

"No anyone could, it's just, most people don't because then you have monthly payments so people can't afford to do it. The few people who have a job just simply don't have the time to look into it." Max stood from the table, "Excuse me I have to go get our money for the night." Max went off and returned a few moments later with several tubes. He gave one to each of us and had two left in his hand. "Now we have one more portion left over we can use for the band. What are you guys thinking?"

Nick spoke out, "how many drops are in there?"

"I told you guys 300 drops each. The extra was because of Dill and they still had us registered with him. The guy who handles the money said it was fine and it's a flaw in the system so he can't change anything until a month and to keep the money."

Jesse was the first to speak, "we should probably use the money on new instruments." Max nodded and we all remembered that our instruments weren't really legal.

Tim questioned this, "Why? We already have them. We should use it on a parties or something."

We all looked at Max. He spoke thoughtfully, "Our instruments are old and we need new ones. This time we will buy a drum set, and then get the rest of you guys new instruments. Maybe one by one so we can have custom made stuff. You will even get a custom made clarinet." Everyone agreed.

When it was time to go Max and Jesse went off. I was going to go with them but decided not to. For some reason Bryan and Nick seemed like they wanted to be alone. They walked off and Tim told me he was going to his room. We were all outside the Red Note; I saw Bryan and Nick walking around the building. Something in me was curious and I followed them at a distance. They weren't heading to their rooms; instead they went all the way behind the lacrosse field. It was almost 10; normally everyone was being kicked off the fields and streets for curfew.

I thought they saw me at one point because they kept looking back as if making sure they were alone. They went behind one of the bleachers and started talking with a man. I tried to see who it was; the face seemed familiar. It was the same guy they were talking to at the Red Note; the same guy with long hair and a mustache. They talked for a while then Bryan and Nick pulled out some drops and handed it to the guy. The guy reached behind him to something on the ground. He came up with two rags and handed it to them. The guy then picked up what was behind him; a small metal box that looked like it belongs to an instrument. The guy took off.

I turned quickly and walked away. It almost felt like I was frozen or something because Bryan and Nick somehow caught up to me and stopped me, "What are you doing out here?" I looked back, Nick seemed nervous as he talked.

"Nothing I just-"

Bryan cut me off, "don't tell anyone."

"Didn't Max tell you not to do this anymore?"

Bryan put his hand on my shoulder, "Look, we took Max's advice; we listened. He said we have to cover our tracks if we do anything like this, just like our instruments. See this guy we talked to covers his tracks well. He's been doing this for two years. He works at the Red Note and has connections. No one can find out. See we meet him here and no one knows."

"Well what did you get exactly?"

Nick answered, "Just some leaves."

"How many leaves? Those bags are pretty big."

Bryan shook his head, "see they fit in my pocket." His pockets bulged enough to be very noticeable.

"How much was all this?"

Nick answered again, "100 drops each." Bryan elbowed him.

"That's a lot of money…"

Bryan sighed, "its not much, and this will last a week. Look, just don't say anything."

"What if you guys get caught? Do you really think I'll let you into our room with that?"

"Alright then, I'll hold onto Nick's if you want; everything ok now?"

"And you think Jesse will be ok with this?"

"Why are you so uptight? No one will know"

"Yes they will. You can smell the stuff outside; but if you leave those in a room for a day it will smell everything up for a month. Anyone walking by the hall will get a face full of that smell."

Bryan seemed to have a rage moment, "Look, we will take care of it. Just keep your mouth shut." Bryan walked off; Nick looked at me, "Nick are you coming?" Nick glanced at the two of us then followed Bryan hiding his head.

The next day Jesse, Bryan and I all had history. This was the history of society with Mr. Barnama. Mr. Barnama walked constantly up and down the rows as he spoke. It almost felt like he had eagle eyes watching you. His room was silent because he was quick to kick someone out if anyone did something wrong. As he walked he told jokes and constantly kept everyone on edge randomly pulling pranks on us that everyone laughed about. He was the only teacher that gave extra credit to help boost our grades if we went to after school events related to his class.

"See when the tribes of the east learned to tame birds, they would send a message to a warring tribe to speak of the terms of a battle." Mr. Barnama looked around the room. "Bryan! Bryan, get up!" Bryan was out cold on the desk. "Class everyone out of the room. Quickly please." Everyone walked out of the room. Mr. Barnama then changed the clocks in the room and closed the shades in the windows so it would look later in the day. He then set an alarm on his desk and walked out of the room. We all looked in the door window; the alarm rang as if class was over. It was so loud we could see the door rattling. Bryan jolted up in confusion; his eyes were red, his hair was unkempt. The alarm stopped; Bryan looked around the empty room. He started picking up his stuff. The alarm rang again louder this time. Bryan was startled and he started running for the door, he dropped some of his books and bumped into everything. When he was close to the door he saw everyone laughing in the window. He looked like a lost puppy and stood there not being awake enough to understand what happen.

Mr. Barnama laughed, "Alright now everyone in the room." We all walked in as Bryan wiped his eyes trying to wake up. "Bryan, get some sleep next time. Don't do this in my class again or I won't be so nice." Bryan clumsily went to pick everything up. We all sat down and Mr. Barnama went on as if nothing happened. "Now class who can tell me the name of the two dominant tribes of this time?" Everyone was silent, Mr. Barnama walked around the room. He slammed a book on one person's desk. "You guys can look up the answers, come on everyone." A handful of students started looking, "Come on, there are enough of you in here to make the pages echo; why are only a few of you looking?"

After class Jesse and I were walking down the hall together; Bryan was farther in front of us. "Max and I went together."

I looked at Jesse, "O, well you guys just disappeared. Where did you go?"

Jesse shrugged, "I went with Max. He said he wanted to see Dill."

"Why, did he apologize or something?"

"No he paid Dill for playing with us that one night then told him that we decided to let him go."

"How did Dill take it?"

"Nothing really, he just took the money and stormed off."

I chuckled, "He got more money than he was supposed to. I bet he's keeping that fancy suit."

"Yea, Max just walked away." we were silent for a moment, "what did you do last night?" I chocked for a second. I could feel Bryan just listening silently; still knowing I wasn't ok with it. Even with Bryan's back turned I could feel his eyes looking at me.

"Oh, nothing really. We just went home after that."

"I would have invited you with us but Max took off too quickly."

"It's fine."

Bryan finally turned to us, "Guys don't forget we are playing today."

"We are?"

I turned to Jesse, "Yea, Max wants to break Tim in a little."

I looked back in front of us and Bryan was gone. I looked back at Jesse, "He really thinks Tim will do us some good."

Later that day we were all in the practice room together; Max wrote a new song and we were trying to work everything out. When we were done Max started talking to Tim. "I didn't think you would catch on that well."

"I try; I mean there's no point in just letting things pass you by right?"

Max put his hand on his chin, "do you happen to know any jokes?"

Tim thought for a moment, "Well I do, would you like to hear one?"

Bryan was shaking his head no. Max smiled, "Go ahead."

Tim straightened himself up. Everyone in the room was ready to see him awkwardly try to entertain us. Tim spoke exaggerating with his hands, He looked uncomfortable but to himself he probably felt relaxed. "I'm not sure if this counts as a joke but it's ironic. One day my partner wanted to have a get together with her friends and asked me if I could host it. So I thought on Thursday me and my friend are always alone in our computer lab doing extra work; so we could invite people as long as nothing happen. Now to me I thought it was just one or two people… but it was really 30. Now when my partner told me who was coming, I thought these people would try to start problems with me. But she convinced me otherwise and asked me to have some music playing. When her friends came they brought all this food and started dancing. My friend and I were scared and hid in an office." Tim chuckled, "it was our first time seeing a get together with popular people and I bet you can see that for our first time this was overwhelming. After an hour my partner came to us and asked why we weren't with everyone else. I told her usually we just did our work then did some live action role play on some of our favorite books we liked." Bryan started chuckling to himself, "She said we should do it still but we said no because everyone would laugh at us. Eventually she told us that it was just like acting and we did it. We grabbed some replica props we made based on the books and started going through the building; we fought and stuck to our roles very nicely I will say."

Tim then started waving his hands around as if reenacting what he did. He acted like he was sword fighting and leaped around the room. Everyone in the room tried to not laugh. "See I thought they would think we were stupid, but they actually liked what we did. Everyone had smiles and cheered and laughed at our book references, they even gave us funny nicknames and talked about us like we were the next big thing with a smile."

Deep down everyone in the room wished they could see this and wanted to hear the jokes they made about Tim. It doesn't seem like Tim really knew what the people at the party really thought. Max spoke, "Do you have any others?"

Tim thought for a moment, "Well I have another. In my cultural studies class, we happened to pick up a book that was used as some barbaric propaganda story and it made a prediction. The barbaric work named *'1984.'* Of course, he embellished it with all these crazy barbaric ideas of a mythical big brother that would cause all these problems. Well that time already passed and the barbaric prediction was of course wrong. I bet the barbarians wished they had a big brother watching them like we have people protecting us."

Everyone in the room awkwardly chuckled looking around at each other. I knew Max didn't want to chuckle but I had a feeling he knew it was risky not to show signs of humor at the failure of the barbarians. Max started speaking, "I have an idea, are you good with remembering things quickly?"

Tim nodded, "I got that song pretty fast didn't I?"

"Well do you think if we gave you some jokes you could do some standup comedy?"

Bryan and Nick glared at Max as if they were ready to kill him. "I might, I haven't been in front of a crowd that much outside of music."

Max smiled, "That's fine, guys write down some jokes and give them to Tim as quickly as you can. Make them good and get as many as you can think of. We have to be on stage in a few."

Nick spoke quickly, "Max what are you planning?"

"We will play the song then have Tim tell some jokes. It will be good; as long as his Jokes are good. If they don't think he's funny than they won't like us as much. Just keep that in mind."

Nick looked at Bryan. Bryan opened his mouth, "Why are we doing this?"

"We haven't had comedy in this school since I was a sophomore. People will like something new coming their way like this. It brings good memories. Plus we will stand out more if Tim is good. We may even get more money."

Bryan and Nick looked skeptical but still wrote down Jokes anyway. Jesse and I put thought into ours. We all handed Tim our Jokes. Tim scanned the jokes, "Ha Ha o some of these are good. Wow that is a good one who wrote this one? Ha the one about the rabbit I'm opening with this one."

Max got our attention, "All right, Tim, you have three minutes. After a while it will start to quiet down then Tim will take the microphone. When Tim is telling jokes, the rest of you have to help him and be alert so you can try to fill in with background music and sounds if you can. Listen to his punch lines."

Jesse turned to Max, "Did you tell the manager about this?"

"No, you guys are the only ones who know." Max walked out of the room.

We all went up on stage. A sound tech stopped us right before it was our time to go on. "What's the name of your group?"

We all looked at Max. The sound tech was waving his hand impatiently for the name. Max spoke, "The Maximus Brothers." The sound tech then turned to the Red Note host for the night and he introduced us to the crowd officially. We all walked onto the stage and started playing. The crowd was getting into the song. We started taking solos and the song started to come to an end. Tim took a solo. Max waved his hand for time; Tim was wiggling along with the music as he played. The crowd laughed at him awkwardly moving around. Tim stopped and Jesse took a drum solo. Tim came forward and got ready to tell his Jokes. Max gave Tim the microphone. Jesse ended his solo and everything stopped suddenly. The crowd seemed confused as if they should cheer or wait for something to happen.

Tim stood in front of the stage. Everyone was watching him. Tim was watching the floor remembering the Jokes. He looked up quickly and started spitting the jokes out one by one. People were laughing at the Jokes while Tim awkwardly walked around the stage speaking. He seemed nervous but at the same time comfortable. Max turned to us and gave us hand signals to play some background music. Bryan started playing a fun song he made up on the spot to help with the atmosphere. Jesse listened for a moment then started playing lightly along to the tune. Bryan turned to Nick and I told us what he was playing. We jumped in and by then Tim seemed to be relaxed and the crowd loved every moment of this.

We had a minutes left and Tim made a final Joke, gave a goodbye and we played a random ending to the song. Somehow it worked out without us planning it. The crowd called our name again and again. We all went behind the curtains as our new fans finally met us. The host of the Red Note that night went up and told the crowd the next time we were scheduled to play.

Max called us, "Guys we are just leaving for tonight. Let's not eat here to keep the crowd hungry for us." Bryan and Nick were praising Tim for his performance as we left out the backdoor.

Tim questioned Max, "Why leave? They love us."

Max smiled, "Yes, this way they would want us again. We shouldn't let them be satisfied. I'll collect the money and meet you guys soon."

Jesse called Max, "So what do we do?"

"Go out to eat just not here."

Jesse turned to everyone, "You guys want to go to that place near the English building?"

We all nodded. Max said, "if you're going to be that close I'll meet you in a few minutes then." Max walked off.

We all went out the back way. When we were outside Bryan turned to Tim, "You did good tonight. Glad you are with us." Nick gave him a pat on the back.

"Really? Was I that good? I thought I did really badly."

Jesse said, "You did good. They really liked you. Just next time we have to plan the song more because that ending was bad."

Bryan chuckled, "Well considering we made it up on the spot, I don't think you could complain much."

We all sat down in the restaurant and ate. Right before we finished Max walked in looking for us. He walked over with a smile. Jesse and I pushed over so he could sit. "Good news." Max handed us our money. "We have been promoted. We only have to perform for two more months to get our name out there; after that we perform once a month and we get more money." We all celebrated; Bryan and Nick were next to Tim patting him on the back for his good work. "Yes, just make sure you guys keep up with your studies and don't waste your money."

Nick turned to Max, "Well we have the money; might as well use it."

Max shrugged, "Well just so you know we keep the money we make here when we leave."

Bryan looked over at Nick and nodded. They stood up from the table. "Where are you guys going?" Max stopped them.

Bryan answered, "We are going down to the football field to see if we can reserve some last minute tickets." I sat there thinking how much of a crafty lie that was.

Max nodded, "Which game are you guys seeing?"

Nick answered, "The B football gym team against the A football gym team."

"I heard people saying it's supposed to be good. Hopefully Mary doesn't want to go."

We chuckled crudely. Bryan and Nick walked away. Jesse turned to us, "Max, what are we doing when you leave?" Max was silent, "What do you think will happen with the Red Note?" Jesse tried again.

Max spoke calmly, "well you guys will just have to take charge. I mean the group will stay around even after we leave. Really we just train the next person to take our places.

The only thing we have to remember is they aren't us and they are them. I mean you guys will have to step it up; you guys will have to train the next generation. If we do it right, the group could last as long as the school exist. Just remember it's easier to train someone when they are young and going to be around for a while instead of people who are older and passing on anyway."

Tim leaned back, "I guess I could takeover when he leaves but after that you guys are on your own."

"Do you think we can start the group backup when we leave this school?" Everyone looked over at me.

Max shrugged, "I only know life here. I know the laws we have to go through when we leave. We might not end up in the same city or our jobs might not be that flexible."

Tim spoke, "How do you know that?"

"I'm in Law class. By Law what we do here in this school determines where we end up when we move on in life, our jobs, homes, cities, and partners."

Teen Hood

      The year came and went; by the end of fall we had our spot at the Red Note secure. The winter felt comfortable, we spent most of our time in the Red Note simply because we had free admission. It almost didn't feel like winter. I managed to pull down my error percentage in class to only five percent; Jesse never dropped below a one percent, Bryan usually stays at four to six percent. Nick on the other hand went from five up to nine percent error. During the winter he never studied and stayed up late to finish last minute things.

      After performances Nick and Bryan would go to the football field then Nick would show up late to room. People loved Tim, everyone wanted to be his friend and invited him places. He changed his glasses to contacts; he dressed differently off stage and blended in with everyone else. He was completely different, still a nerdy computer tech but now he had confidence. He looked like a different person; even his partner seemed different. She looked happier to be with him. When the spring came around Nick dropped to ten percent error. He skipped as many classes as he could wit out getting in trouble. The summer is the only different part of the year. The first part of the summer is normal classes. The middle is special exams and the last month is our break. The seniors are leaving this week.

      It's our last week with Max. We didn't get to see him much because he was taking some jobs requirement exams. Today we finally get to see Max. Tomorrow is the senior ceremony when they graduate, then next week we take our pre-citizens test. "So do you know where you are going from here?"

      Max turned to me; we were all sitting in a field around Max. Max was on a bleacher next to Tim. On the floor was

Jesse, Bryan Nick and I. Max leaned back, "Yes, I am going to be with Mary in a class for home in a IQN place."

Nick was the only one who didn't know what Max said, "What's an IQN place?"

"Isolated and quiet neighborhood."

Nick spoke again, "there are different class houses?"

Max nodded, "yes, one to twenty."

Bryan spoke, "how do we get into good places?"

"Well, your neighborhood depends on your job and personality. People who are quiet and not social are placed accordingly. Your house depends on your job, personality and need of space and code of conduct. If you job requires you to need an office you get one. If you have hobbies and can provide proof of you prosper in it, you get rooms for that. It's averaged between you and your partner to determine your home."

Jesse spoke next, "So what does your house have?"

Max thought for a moment, "Well for me an office, music, art, cooking; for Mary swimming, office and dancing room. I'm going to work for the government, over viewing Laws; Mary is going to be a dancing instructor. She didn't have a good conduct because of her freshmen year but she 'improved' after that. But because of my reputation and conduct," he paused as if making a dramatic effect, "our house will have 4 bed rooms; one for us, we get a servant and two guess rooms. A large kitchen, pool, 4 bathrooms a storage room, two garages and six large empty rooms for us to use at will."

Jesse shook his head, "That's a lot. It probably would have cost 100,000 drops. Do you have to pay for furniture? And what are the empty rooms for?"

Max nodded, "The house is actually 250,000 drops. We get a basic set of furniture that we have to spend drops if we want to replace it; but the empty rooms are for whatever we want. Ideally they are for our hobbies. More than likely we will find other things to do with the rooms. I mean I'm good at art but it's not something I would spend that many drops on."

Tim turned, "so you got the room for art and you are not going to use it?"

"No, I'm going to use the room I just don't need that much for it. I mean my art grade has been excellent. I'm just not going to invest that much into it. I just want to keep my art in my sketch book."

Bryan got Max's attention, "So what is happening at the ceremony tomorrow?"

"Well basically we are going to the entertainment center. They call off the names of each senior; they come up grab some paper and walk off."

Nick made a face, "That's it? And we have to sit through it all?"

Tim nodded unenthusiastically. Max spoke, "yes, they always call the Law and government jobs first; then science and on and on. It's kind of funny. We hear a speech; people walk across a stage and then we just get on with our lives. After I walked across the stage they will shake my hand and I can leave and do whatever I want until the bus picks us up at the end of the ceremony."

Nick spoke, "And we can't leave after you walk?"

Tim shook his head as if he was annoyed. Bryan stood up, " If this is our last day, then let's spend it well. We can go to the Red Note and order some cake. We should end the day with a mini party just us."

Everyone smiled and we all went down to the Red Note. While we were in there, people were already partying and having a great time. The building felt so alive with welcoming faces. The band was playing music that just made you want to move. Max, Tim, Bryan Jesse Nick and I all sat at one back table. A waiter brought us food and we pigged out. I almost felt bad because we left the biggest mess all over the table and floor. This wasn't something we normally did but the place was so happy and the janitors didn't seem to mind. The night continued on, we danced for hours. When the Red Note was just a half hour from closing we ordered a cake. The waiter brought it over with a dull cake knife. We all went around exchanging stories about Max and how much of an amazing person he was. Most of Bryan and Nick stories were how Max kept them from trouble.

When it was all over we had to pay a really large bill. "Max we can all chip in. you don't have to pay."

Max leaned in and turned to Jesse, "Guys it's been amazing being with you all; and I know how this is supposed to all be about me. But I want to give back to you guys. I don't need the money. I'll pay for it." Max went in and called over a waiter. He told the waiter he needed money out of his account. The waiter pointed to a computer-banking machine. Max went over and pulled out the whole price, then poured out all the drops he had on the table. He turned to us and smiled, "Come on, guys lets go home."

As we left I noticed Nick went off. He was talking to the same guy from the football field. I went over to let him know we were leaving. He looked at me with an eye and said he would be at the dorm later. I walked away and met up with the others.

Max turned to me, "where is Nick?"

"He said he had to take care of something and would meet up with us later."

Tim had a small engineering manual in his hand. "It's been a good time working with you."

Max turned to him, "No thank you. Without you putting you self all out there, we wouldn't be here."

Tim smiled, "yea but you gave me a chance. Everyone who looked at me before didn't take me serious."

Max shrugged, "I learned something in life." We all waited for him to speak.

Bryan went ahead, "What's that?"

Max turned to him, "Well I learned nothing can stop you from your dreams."

Bryan and Tim acted like they heard this before. Jesse thought then spoke, "That must be something everyone has to learn."

Max smiled, "Yes, but few people ever understand." We all looked at him, "Most people just look at something they want and see it as if it's there in front of them. Dreams and goals are something that maybe one day you will get there if you are lucky. It's always a fuzzy thought."

Bryan chuckled, "That tends to be the common idea of it."

Max nodded, "Yes and that's not it. You have to look past what you see. I realized that really you are just a step away from any goal at any moment." Max stopped and turned to us, "You know we cause ninety percent of the problems we go through. The rest are smaller problems we generally don't see affecting us. Guys just know that as long as you always try and always put you're fullest into anything you can always make it. Don't sit around and let life pass you by. Start preparing for your future even before your future is possible. You are really only limited by the natural constant laws of the universe; which don't change and even we don't know them all yet. Just remember to always keep pushing through no matter how hard things get. If something is hard, that means you don't understand it. It will only be hard until you learn how to understand it. I realized that the only thing that separates you from anything in life is simply your will and drive to see it. Money, education, social state, nothing can stop you. Only you can. I want you guys to remember that."

We all nodded our heads. Bryan and Tim went off to their rooms. Jesse and I waited a moment. "Max, what is your goal?"

He turned to me, "I want to fix the law and the problems we have. I'm going to be changing the future. Soon the laws of men we follow will be things we can handle and won't accuse us." We nodded and went our separate ways.

Tonight people were up late. As I went back to my room, I saw people laughing and partying the night away. Normally we were all supposed to stay quiet at night, but now no one seemed to care. When I made it to the room I went straight to bed.

Sometime in the night Nick came in the room. He opened the door and the light from the hallway woke me. I opened one eye trying to keep the brightness from hurting. Nick walked in clumsily eating a large slice of cake. "You're still eating?"

"Shut up!" Nick walked into the middle of the room. He took off his shoes and took a large bite of his cake.

"Where have you been?"

"Shut up!" Nick hopped up onto his bed.

"You're just going to leave the door open?"

"Be quiet already!" he spoke as if crumbs were flying out his mouth. I picked myself up and closed the door.

The Ceremony started early in the day; everyone had until 11:30 to eat and do what they needed and by 12 everyone was supposed to be at the entertainment center already seated. The stands were full with a handful of teacher's walking around. Everyone was sitting in section according to their class. Tim was on some other half of the stands; Bryan, Nick, Jesse and I were above the first five rows. In front of us was a railing with a walking way. Off to the side was an entrance.

The ceremony already started and we were at the end of a speech; we were all sitting in our seats when the speech was done. The person giving the speech then changed what he was saying; "Now we will call off all the people who will be moving on in life with the job they will undergo." He called the first several jobs and the people who were getting those jobs. Everyone was standing and clapping. The four of us started silently lean on the railing waiting for Max's name. Nick seemed fidgety while we waited.

The people walked across the stage, the speaker gave some of them a metal and others a rolled up paper. Bryan and Nick were whispering back and forth. I couldn't hear over everyone clapping. We all weren't paying much attention but everyone else seemed to be interested. We tried to find a way to pass the time until the speaker announced the Law over seeing office. We all stood up and waited excitingly over the railing. The speaker said, "Max Liphdom."

We all cheered and shouted as Max walked across the stage. Our cheering was even heard over every one's clapping. Max smiled as he walked trying not to act like he heard us. The speaker had a metal in his hand. When Max was in front of him the speaker pinned the metal to Max's shirt over his heart. A teacher came over and told us all to stop cheering. Max then turned and bowed. He bowed in our direction then walked off the stage. We clapped again when the teacher was gone as Max disappeared.

Nick backed up from the railing. Bryan turned, "Where are you going?"

Nick was fidgety, "I'm going to see Max."

Jesse spoke, "We can't leave until it's over."

"All the teachers are here no one will know." Nick went off.

Bryan ran after him, "I swear if you're doing something stupid-" Jesse and I looked at each other then went to see if everything was ok.

Nick went through an exit and turned a corner. Jesse and I sped up to meet Bryan. We were in a long hallway; at the end was a staircase. Nick ran down the stairs. We followed him down and he took a turn. Nick ran faster around the corner and slammed into Max. We turned a corner to find Max and Nick on the floor. Bryan and I walked over to help them get up.

"What are you guys doing here?" Max grabbed my hand as I helped him up.

Bryan spoke, "We were trying to catch Nick." Max turned to Nick and glared.

Nick was scratching himself unusually, "I'm sorry I came to find you."

Max sighed, "You guys have to stay out of trouble. This isn't how you do it. If someone finds you guys here we could get in big trouble." We all hung our heads in shame. "Well come on guys let's get back to your seats, hopefully no one will notice. Since you're with me they might let this slide."

We all went back up the stairs as Max escorted us. We continued down the hallway and turned a corner. "Do you guys smell that?"

We all sniffed the air. I turned to Jesse, "it smells pretty grosse." Bryan looked like he was frozen for a moment. Max started to rush us, "We have to go now, hurry up, come on."

We all walked faster and then we seen Mr. Barnama walking down the hall with two men in black. He turned angrily and seen us, "Hey, what are you all doing there?"

Max stopped us all, he then turned, "Guys we can't be caught with this smell." Mr. Barnama started running in our direction while the men in black didn't notice and kept walking. Nick started sprinting down the hall trying not to be seen.

Mr. Barnama yelled, "Stop!" we all ran faster down the hallway following Nick. I turned back and seen Mr. Barnama pause at where we were and started smelling the air; then continued after us. We all ran down the stairs and turned a corner. Nick called to us, "Bathroom's over here." As I passed the corner I saw Mr. Barnama sliding down the railings on the stairs like a super soldier.

The moment I was around the corner two arms grabbed me and pulled me into the bathroom. The door closed and Bryan locked it while I was on the ground. I looked up; we were in the middle of a single person bathroom, one toilet and one sink with a mirror and hand-dryer. Max was by the sink with his head in his hands. Bryan was blocking the door while Jesse was standing next to me helping me up. Nick was sitting on the toilet feedling around with a small brown bag. Bryan came up from the door, "What are you doing!" We all looked at Bryan, "You better not light that stuff in here!" We all looked at Nick; he shrugged and popped some shredded leaves into his mouth and started chewing.

Bryan walked over and grabbed the bag; Nick struggled to keep it. Max turned to them, "Guys, it's a single bathroom. You can hear everything outside." Bryan and Nick stopped struggling and stayed quiet. Max came up from the sink with his hands on his face. He then sat on the floor and waved his hand telling us to sit. We all looked at him funny. He waved his hand again. Jesse and I went down to see what he had planned. Bryan and Nick then came over and we made a close circle. Max leaned in closely, "We have to get out of here without anyone knowing. Where is the closest exit?"

Nick blurted out, "There is one right outside."

We all went in unison "shhhhhhhhhh!"

Jesse spoke softly, "there are teachers standing there to let people go to the restroom."

Bryan interrupted, "What if someone has to go to the bathroom?" a feeling of hopelessness filled the room.

Max thought for a moment, "This could be it. I mean just hold the door and hope no one comes in. we will have to wait till it's over and we can hopefully slip out with the crowd. My bus won't leave right away." Max stood up and went by the sink. We all froze for a moment then Jesse went to the door. The door made a thud as if someone tried to get in. Max turned, "I'm in here!" the person sounded like they stopped trying. Max brought us together, "where is the bag?"

There was a banging at on the door, "Come out now! You don't have permission to use this restroom." Nick handed the bag to Max. Max stuffed it in his pants and leaned in close to us, "wait until it sounds safe then leave when you can."

Max went over to the door and slipped out carefully so whoever was outside couldn't see inside. The door closed behind him; Mr. Barnama spoke, "Well, Well, Max. You were a good law student; you even *had* a bright future. Come with me." We heard the metal being unpinned from his shirt. We were silent as footsteps slowly faded. Every one's face was like stone.

After a moment we all looked at Nick. "What? Why are you looking at me?"

Bryan ran at him and held him to the wall, "I told you not to be stupid!" We ran over to hold back Bryan, "Look what you did!" we held him back and Nick dropped to the floor without a word. "You can't tell me you don't have any emotions with this!" Bryan struggled to come after Nick. We continued to hold back Bryan and after a while he stopped. Bryan just stormed out of the bathroom. Jesse and I looked at each other and tried to sneak out quickly. We went out together and acted causally. Dill called us "is the bathroom finally open?" We paused.

Jesse answered, "Almost." Nick walked out and disappeared. I looked back and Dill stared at us with anger. Jesse and I found a way back to our seats without being caught. We sat back in our seats and the speaker gave a closing speech; "You don't think Dill will say anything, do you?"

I looked at Jesse, "Well, I doubt he will go out of his way to; but we kind of dropped him." We sat there in silence. The speech was over and everyone was dismissed. I turned and saw Bryan sitting in an empty row above us. He had his face covered and was rock solid.

Jesse was about to start walking out with everyone else, "Wait, and let's try to get everyone together." We waited until everyone was gone then went over to Bryan, "Hey it's time to go." Bryan was motionless.

Jesse tapped his shoulder, "it's time to go." Bryan picked his head up; his face was red. He stood and we all walked out together. Bryan was silently strolling behind us.

"So, what are we going to do at the Red Note?"

Jesse thought, "Well I guess we are going to have to find someone new, unless we can get some special arrangement."

"You think it will be easy?"

"Because of Tim we aren't a normal performance."

"Yea, but other comedians are coming up."

"None as good as Tim. Plus we are his band and we help with his act."

That night I was sitting in my room, playing guitar. Nick walked in the room; his eyes were red. He slammed the door behind him. "Where have you been?"

Nick walked over to his desk, "I was out."

"You don't look well." Nick was stumbling through some drawers. He pulled out some eye drops and some fixer sticks. Then Nick went down and pulled out a small bag of crackers from under his desk. He sat down and started eating, "Did you talk to Jesse and Tim?"

Nick glared at me, "No why?"

"Tim told me he was going to talk to the guys at the Red Note." Nick shrugged and stuffed down some more crackers. The door thudded with 3 bangs. Nick and I looked at each other. The bangs went off again. "You might want to put more drops in your eyes." Nick started watering his eyes with drops while I went to the door.

Two large men in black stood behind the head of the student health department. "Hello gentlemen, I am sorry to bother you. It seems there was an issue that occurred today and your presence is needed to resolve it. Please take what you need and come with me."

The department head walked away from the door and waited for us. The men in black held the door open. I walked over to Nick, "Are you ready?" Nick put down the crackers and stood up. We calmly walked out of the room.

The head of the department looked at us, "Very well; let's get going." he started walking down the hall. The department head walked stiffly. As we passed each room I noticed almost everyone was already sleeping. Usually you could see the light from the room slipping under the door; but almost everyone was off. When we came outside there was a vehicle with opened doors waiting for us. There were two rows of seats lined up against the sides. We went in and everything closed behind us. Inside everything was dark except for a light on the ceiling.

Nick and I sat across from each other. Nick was staring at the floor absently. The vehicle moved and we were motionless. The vehicle went over some bumps then after a few minutes we came to a stop. It happened and two men in black suits were waiting for us. We stepped out and looked around. There was a building to the left and to the right was a wall, in front of us was another wall. I couldn't tell where we came to or what this place was. The men in black walked us into the building; there was a long white hallway, on the ceiling were long strips of lights, each of the doors looked like a mirror. The floor was black but seemed glossy.

The men took us around a corner and stopped in front of a door. We walked over to it and the door opened. Max, Bryan and Jesse were on the other side sitting in some kind of waiting room. We walked in; the walls were maroon, there was a glass table with a metal frame in the center of the place. Around the table were brown couches.

Nick and I sat down and the door closed behind us. We sat and looked at each other for a moment. A person then walked in with some pastries and left them on the table. When we were alone Max spoke, "They can't hear us in here but they can see us." he reached over and grabbed a pastry. "They are interested in how guilty we appear. It's a mental game from here on." he smiled and tried to cheer us up.

Jesse spoke, "So you know what's happening?"

"Sophomore year they teach you about school procedures. When they found me they searched me and found the leaves. You guys must have been spotted by someone."

Bryan sighed, "Why did Dill have to be there!"

"Yea, see they normally they do a full scale investigation on any incident. They question all witnesses even if they are just by standers."

Jesse continued, "So since Dill happened to be the one going to the bathroom at that time he was questioned by Law?"

"Now you are getting it, based on what he said they will already determine our judgment and how they question us."

"What will happen after questions?"

Max turned to me, "no matter what we are all flagged as problem people. You will always be watched closely and this will always be on your record." Nick finished eating the food and licked his lips. "Worst possible outcome is we are all deemed as Law breakers; from there I don't know what happens to those people. They never told us."

Bryan jumped in, "and how do we stay out of trouble."

Max chuckled, "I told you all this before; but in this case we need the same exact story. It needs to seem as harmless as possible for you guys. There isn't much I can do because if we tell the truth I will be aiding criminals. If we have a different story I was the one with drugs, breaking the law, and Nick and you all can go free, possibly. You all have a chance, but just one."

Jesse spoke, "either way you are a Law breaker. So what should we do?"

Max took a deep breath, "The story was; you guys are my friends but never knew I had a problem, say it like that, exactly like that. You are freshman and simply didn't know you couldn't walk around. You ran into me, scared because I was chewing; when Mr. Barnama came by you guys were scared and ran off and followed me because you didn't know what to do"

Bryan had an angry look, "Why? You didn't do Anything, you shouldn't have to do this."

Max tried to continue, "I walked out with the bag. I helped you guys escaped because I didn't want you guys getting wrapped up in my problem. There is nothing that can be done for me, you all have a chance."

"So, Nick should get away with this!" Nick had a blank expression at Bryan as if he was innocent.

Max shook his head, "Can't do that, see, they find out about Nick, they will do more investigations and find out about you. You dug yourself into this hole as well, Nick's not alone in this." The room felt humbled at Max's words.

"If they do investigation on me, they can't do anything. The only thing they can do is track me to the bag. They can't find the origin of the bag unless someone tells them it's not yours."

Max stopped himself; "See my story was, I got the bag from one of the patches of plants growing in the woods. Since people grow plants in random places around the campus they will never know."

Bryan shook his head, "Max I won't do it. There must be some way to get you out of this."

Max stopped himself, "Just carry out my last wish. Don't waste your lives, try to help anyway you can. This world shouldn't be this way."

A man in black walked into the room. "We would like to call you each one by one starting with Nick. Who is Nick?" we all pointed as if accusing him. Nick was sleeping on the couch as if he was at home. The man in black didn't pay attention, "Very well, the next person is Bryan. Please come with me and wake him up." Bryan stood up and left.

Jesse turned to Max, "it's been a pleasure knowing you."

Max smiled, "This might not be the end."

I called Max, "You seem happy, why? Everything you worked for, leading up to this moment was a waste?"

Max shook his head; "The only thing that can stop you from your dreams is you."

Another man in black came in and called my name. I stood and followed him down the hallway and he stopped in front of a room. I walked in by myself and seen a metal table in the center of a black room with one light shining on a chair next to the table. I sat down and waited. Two guys walked in; they both had dress up shirts and vests; one had spiky hair and the other looked like a professor.

"Hello," The professor walked in front of me while the guy with spiky hair walked around in a circle. "I know you must be confused as to why you are here. Let me explain before we go on." The man started speaking with his hands while the men with spiky hair continued walking. "It seems Max has been found in possession of illegal drugs. We have reported that you and your friends were in the same room Max was found in. are you friends with Max?"

"Yes, I am."

"Have you known him for a long time? If so, how long?"

"Since I came to this school."

"Have you noticed anything about his personality that would suggest actions like this about him?"

"Not that I remember."

The guy with spiky hair leaned in closely, "you don't remember? I suggest you try harder." He continued walking.

"I don't think there was anything that stood out."

"You think? You must know unless you're hiding something-" He shook the chair, "Are you?"

"No, he didn't seem like he was that kind of person."

"Better."

The professor spoke, "Why did you and your friends leave during the event?" I thought for a moment wondering if Bryan stuck to the story. The man with spiky hair pushed the chair, "Why? Did you hear the question?"

"I don't know why they did, but I didn't know we couldn't leave. I simply followed thinking we were going for a walk."

The professor spoke, "Did you know Max had any illegal plants before this event?"

Before the man with spiky hair could say anything I blurted out, "No, I didn't know."

"Why then did you run from Mr. Barnama?"

The guy with spiky hair pushed the seat forward, "Did you have a reason to be scared?"

"I was just scared."

"Why were you scared?" he stood in my face, "Did you know something? Innocent has no fear of judgment."

"I don't know there was a smell and then I heard a voice saying run and I saw-"

"Do you know that smell? Answer the question!"

"No, it was strange to me."

"Where did it come from?"

"It just filled the air."

"You know that smell don't you?"

"No I don't."

"Then why did you run when you smelt that smell?"

"I ran when someone said to."

"Who said to?"

"I don't remember!"

"Yes you do! You just don't want to remember!" he rocked the chair.

The professor stopped him, "Let him be." the man with spiky hair continued walking around. "We have another issue at hand. Do you remember Dill? Dill Maborn?"

"Yes I have met him."

"He was in your music group for some time?"

"He was, yes."

"He claimed your group gathered in a storage house. Is this true?"

I thought quickly, "I don't recall."

"It was on the east side of the campus."

"I remember Max mentioning he owned it for some time. I do not recall anything after that."

The guy with spiky hair shook the chair, "Yes you do, don't lie!"

The professor shook his hand out, "Easy, where did you and your music group practice before you received your job at the Red Note."

I thought quickly, "We accompanied Jesse in the open room nights in the music building many times."

"Where did you and your friends get your musical abilities from?"

"Well I was interested in music back in the virtual world. I played guitar in my free time and I thought maybe it would be the same."

"You never took a music course? Is that correct?"

"Yes."

"So where did you get your instrument?"

I put out a strange look. The man with spiky hair pushed the chair, "Where did your guitar come from?"

"What do you mean?"

"Don't act innocent, where did the guitar come from?"

"I paid for it and registered it at the music department."

The guy with spiky hair looked at the professor. The professor spoke as if stunned, "And how long ago did you say this happen?"

"Some time after performing at the Red Note."

"Sorry that is not the instrument we meant. We are talking about the one you used before the Red Note."

I thought quickly again, "I took out guitars from the music department often."

The guy with spiky hair got in my face, "That wouldn't have been enough. What else did you do?"

"I didn't do anything other than that-" I paused.

"You did what?"

"I borrowed some from a friend if they would let me."

"How long!"

"Maybe a night or two."

The professor stopped him, ""That's enough. Let him be. Today, what happen when you were all in the bathroom?

"Nothing-"

The man with spiky hair got in my face, "Nothing? Max was found with some chewing leaves and you're saying nothing? What happened in that restroom?"

"We were scared and someone pulled me-"

"You were scared? Innocents don't fear judgment."

"I didn't know what would happen."

"And Max told you something in there what was it?"

"Nothing he just-"

"It was something"

"No we just-"

"We just, we just, out with it!"

The professor stopped him, "Ok enough! Just tell me what happened."

I opened up to the professor, "Max just explained to us how he had the plants and said he would turn himself in. I had no part in anything."

The professor sat back, "One more question." I sat back trying to catch my nerves, "At any time, was there anyone else in your group who might have showed signs that they were on plants?"

"Not that I can recall."

The man with spiky hair spoke from behind me, "Yes, you can. You and your friends were part of the gym class back in the beginning of the year, they had high leaves content in their system; you recall that now don't you?"

"I don't know, I can only speak for myself."

"Why can't you speak on behalf of your friends?"

"Because I can't lie and say I witness what I haven't."

They both backed up a little. The professor waved and a man in the back walked into the room. I instinctively knew I was supposed to follow him. He took me to another waiting room. This one was smaller than the last. It just had one chair in it, next to a coffee table. I waited there for what felt like ten dreadful minutes. I sat there wondering how everyone else was doing; Bryan might have told on Nick, Nick might be too out of it to keep the story, who knows what Jesse will do.

Another man in black then came in the room. I followed him outside to the same vehicle I was brought in; Jesse, Nick and Bryan were already there. They looked at me then stood up. I looked back and Max was by the door with a man in front of him. They put handcuffs on Max while the man in black told me to keep moving. I walked on and as I sat down with the man in black next to me; Max looked at us. His face was like stone, he had no expression. He looked away from us as the vehicle closed and took off.

The ride back was awkward. The man watched us the whole way; no one dared to speak. Before the first stop the man spoke in a calm voice, "I know you are all tired, just know this was for your safety."

The first stop was my place. Nick and I walked out; the moon was up in the sky, the sun was just barely showing its light in the sky; the stars were barely visible for some reason. Nick and I walked to our room. I opened the door and Nick closed it behind him.

"Did they question you?"

Nick looked at me yawning, "What?"

"Did they question you?"

"Yes."

"What did you say?"

"I just told them I was innocent."

"You think Max will be ok?"

"No idea, but we are free."

"Is that how you see it? He gave his life for you and you don't even seem to care"

He yawned "Yup."

"That's it?" he didn't answer, "Nick?" no response, "Nick?"

The next Day I dragged myself out of bed after sleeping in. Nick's bed was empty. I got dressed and went to see Bryan and Jesse. Everyone from school was up and about. People were happy and joyful. When I came to their room, I knocked and waited a minute; no answer. I knocked again; Bryan opened the door. He had an angry look. He walked away from the door and sat on his bed. The floor was a mess with clothes. I walked in and closed the door behind me. The lights were off, "Are you guys decorating?"

Jesse called me, "He's mad about yesterday."

"So you just threw things around?" Bryan didn't answer.

"He's not in the mood."

I looked at Jesse, "This is going to be something to clean."

"It's fine, it's all his stuff anyway."

The air in the room felt heavy and sad. Bryan had his hands over his face. He called me, "Where's Nick?"

"No idea, he just took off."

Bryan picked up his head and seemed even angrier. "I know where he is." he started getting ready. Jesse joined him.

We followed Bryan to a place behind the botany building. There were piles of dead plants all organized behind a green house. Everything looked like a maze; Bryan navigated it with ease. He turned around a large pile of plants; Nick was lying comfortably against a bundle of plants. He made himself a large cigar of leaves. He sucked on his creation and puffed a smoke ball into the air.

"What are you doing!"

Nick looked at us with a smile, "I'm making faces in the air." He puffed again, "this one looks like one of the guys we seen last night." his eyes were red; he looked like he couldn't tell where up or down was. Bryan went and stood just before him.

"Are you kidding me right now?" Nick didn't listen, "Max just died saving your life and you're just going to sit there? You don't even care!"

Nick smiled, "I'm just doing what you showed me; and Max did this so I could live my life. I'm doing what he wanted, aren't I?"

"No, he died so we can continue on; so we can have a chance at life. Not throw everything away."

"You and Max both taught me to cover my tracks. That's what I'm doing. No one will know."

"Max showed us how to stay out of the penalty of the law.

"So? You did the same thing?"

Bryan's face was red and he tensed up. Jesse went in as Bryan attacked Nick. We held him back before he could lay a hand on Nick. We pulled him back; Nick let out a puff of smoke. Bryan started to calm down and took a deep breath and started walking off.

"What are we going to do about our performance at the Red Note?"

Bryan answered me without turning, "I'll be there."

Jesse and I looked at each other and walked away from Nick. We went to a bench somewhere away so we could talk.

"So we can still perform without Max?"

Jesse knotted, "Tim and I talked to the manager before we were taken last night. He said since we are the second highest rank we can get away with it."

"I smiled, "they probably just don't want to lose one of their biggest groups."

"Yea, don't look all suspicious, but is there a person over by the pole looking at us? Let's walk."

We got up and arranged ourselves so I could see. Most of the adults were out in their own place; the only ones still around us were the ones that had to be around, disciplinarians, doctors and such. I noticed this person only watched us and tried not to seem like it. "You think that's them watching us?"

Jesse knotted, "I noticed him walking over a minute ago. It probably took them sometime to find someone to monitor us."

"Nick is going to get catch quickly."

"I doubt it."

"Why's that?"

"I was talking with Bryan and we think they think Nick is completely innocent."

"How? His grades dropped, he spends a lot of time alone. They must be tracking his money."

"He doesn't use the schools banking system. They don't know that; and his alone time is probably compensated with the fact that he likes attention and is always entertaining people at the Red Note every night."

"What about his grades?"

"They dropped but the teachers like him. He showed me a test once and he should have an eleven percent error but the teacher gave him an eight percent error simply out of favoritism."

"So why are we suspicious then?"

"Not sure, but looks like we will have to deal with this for the rest of our lives."

Later that day we all met at the Red Note. Bryan didn't even look in the direction of Nick. Turns out during our questioning we all said the same basic thing. Except for Nick. He wouldn't tell us anything that happened. Tim showed up late and we did our performance without Max. We just let Tim have even more time for his jokes. We did this so perfectly that no one even knew anything about what happen last night. Not even Tim. Tim started off explaining about how Max graduated and how we would all miss him; and with that life moved on.

    The time came for us to take our pre-citizens test. In the morning everyone had a knock at the door with a man handing out letters. The letters told us the time and place we had to take our test. Mine was one of the first tests; one o clock at the Law building, room 123.

    The letter explained the process and said that the test would help place us in classes for the next schooling season. At one point it talked about the match making part of the test. My test was at the same time as Bryan's. We met up and walked down to the place. There were two lines leading into the building; one for men and one for woman. Bryan and I waited patiently while the line moved slowly.

    I overheard some guys talking in front of me, "Yea, I heard that everyone gets their partner after the test ends and we stay with them for life."

    "Well this girl better be worth the test."

    "I know, she better not be stupid or anything, have you seen some of the girls around?"

    I turned and heard some of the girls having a conversation, "You're joking right? How do we get a good looking guy?"

    "You have to answer the right questions."

    "My man better be strong, good looking and have a good job."

    Bryan wasn't in the mood to speak. When we came into the building a table was set up for us to register for the test. A junior, now a new senior, was at the table to explain the process and help us register. He helped me register and told me to go to my assigned room. The room was the size of a small office. I walked in and a junior law student walked in wearing a suit.

    "Hello, during the test you will be alone. Every answer is your personal conclusion. Don't feel pressured because nothing will count against you." He walked over and placed a paper stake on a desk in the room. The paper stake looked like two small books. "Please answer all questions in both sections. Remove the sealing tape on the test booklet as carefully as you can." He placed several pencils on the desk and walked out saying, "you have up to two hours to finish."

    I sat in the desk and looked at the test booklet; one was greenish-blue, the other was a golden-tan. On the cover of each was a large grid with areas to bubble and fill out information. The ten booklets was the first one on top. I opened to the first page; holding the booklet closed was a sticker an inch long across the lose pages. I split the sticker carefully, peeled it back and looked at the format. Each page was double sided; multiple choices, on the side was a column to bubble in answers. I picked up a pencil and started the first question:

    1) Pretend you were in this situation; an animal you never seen before was on the side of the road and looked like it was about to die soon. What do you do?
a) Find a way to put it down with brute force
b) Find a way to put it down painlessly
c) Comfort the animal until it dies
d) Examine the animal to see if you can save it
e) Examine it to learn more about it
f) Ignore it and keep walking

The second question followed the same format:

    2) … There was a school bully people knew about. You see the bully picking on someone. What do you do?
a) Help the bully
b) Help defend the victim
c) Watch and cheer it on
d) Watch and stay silent
e) Watch then tell an authority later
f) Tell an authority right away

13) ... If a dog was stuck by some ascendant and couldn't go free. What would you do?
a) Find a way to force the dog out
b) Find a way to remove what was around the dog
c) Call for help
d) Tease the dog
e) Stay and comfort the dog
f) Pretend it's not there and move on

During the test I kept thinking about what Max told me so long ago. It was true; most of the questions just seemed to get into your head so they could see how barbaric you were.

33) ... you hear someone reading out loud from a book. It sounds like the book promotes barbaric ideas. What do you do?
a) Continue listening to the story with care
b) Want to read it yourself
c) Challenge the ideas being said
d) Tell the person to stop reading
e) Report the person
f) Do nothing

The more I thought about it the more I wanted to go back and change my answers. For Jesse, Bryan and I, maybe even Nick, it was more important that we had 'good' scores on this exam however they reviewed the answers. At one point it felt like my life depended on the answers. After I finished, I carefully bubbled in everything hoping I put the right answers. I pushed the booklet aside and took a deep breath. I then picked up the booklet and started again. This one felt friendlier, all the questions in it made you want to answer and it was even fun. While taking the text I wondered; these questions asked you for your opinions and preferences. In class they always said we aren't supposed to be an individual. I thought to myself, how can we get rid of 'barbaric ideas' if they made us human?

1) Which of the following would describe your life, as you know it?
a) A roller coaster

b) Historical
c) An adventure
d) Lonely
e) Frustrating
f) Average

...5) you would rather enjoy what kind of atmosphere?
a) Lost of thing to stimulate interest
b) Peace and quiet
c) Competitive
d) Welcoming
e) Organized
f) Any

...12) in regards to people you...
a) Would rather have tones of people to interact with
b) Have people around without interaction
c) Can deal with anything
d) Would rather have time for yourself
e) Have no human interaction
f) Anything is fine

...13) for a job you would rather be?
a) Doing hard work
b) Making creative ideas for others
c) Managing things
d) Work under directions
e) Away from people
f) Anything is fine

...20) Over all you like to dress?
a) Extravagant
b) Fancy
c) Average
d) Causal
e) Relaxed

f) Depends on occasion

...47) you would be most interested in?
a) Athletics things
b) Language arts
c) Other arts
d) Intellectual topics
e) Human studies
f) Anything
Around question 60 is where it came down to what everyone was waiting for.;

...61) If you had to live in a place you would want it to be?
a) As big and luxurious as possible
b) Higher class
c) Average
d) Smaller and humble
e) Just what you need to live nothing more
f) Anything is fine

...70) Your partner should be?
a) Rich and well known
b) Above average wealth
c) Average
d) Blow average
e) Just what they need no more
f) Money doesn't matter

71) Your partner's personality should ?
a) Be the center of attention
b) Be social butterfly

c) Be a by stander
d) Not like attention
e) Be anti-social
f) Be how they are

72) Your partner should dress?
....
73) Your partner should look?
....
74) Your partner should act
....

    The questions went on and started getting more and more personal. The answers even started to seem like they shouldn't be on a formal test. When I finished I took another deep breath. I placed the booklet aside knowing that whatever I answered would be final. I stood up and went to the door. A junior was standing outside and looked at me when I came out.
    "Have you finished your test?"
    "Yes I have."
    "I will take your test material, please wait a moment." He went into the room then came out with a paper with some number on it. "Please take this paper down to room eleven. Tell them you finished your exam and hand them this. Your results will come by the end of the next week. Enjoy the rest of your day."
    He handed it to me and I went on my way. Outside the room was a short line of men all waiting outside the door. The line moved slowly. When I finally came in to the room there were two nurses with two seats set up. I walked up to one of the nurses and she reached out her hand. I gave her the paper and she then went to grab a test tube, "please take a seat." She then wrote the number on the tube and started taking some of my blood. "This sample will be submitted along with your test scores, have a great day."

I walked out of the building and headed over to the Red Note knowing Bryan would be there. The bouncer out front let me in with a smile. Bryan was sitting at a back table alone. He was staring at a tall glass of apple cider. I sat across from him, "What did you think of the test?"

Bryan sighed, "I finished it."

"No other comments on it?"

"Not yet."

"What's wrong?"

"What's wrong? What do you mean what's wrong? Max is probably off to some prison or his body being burn to ashes. He just wasted the most potential he had all for us and Nick, who doesn't even care."

"Well all we have to do is control Nick or change his mind or something."

"You think he will listen?"

"Well there isn't any point in staying in a rut-"

"Trust me I don't plan too." Bryan chugged his glass and walked off.

Today was the day we all got our results back from the test. In the morning someone knocked on our door. I answered it and a junior from law class was at the door with tubes in a bag. "Are you the person living here? You live with a Nick right?"

"I am, yes."

The guy reached into his bag and pulled out a white tube a foot long. "These are your full names correct?"

"Yes" He handed the tubes to me and took off. I walked over and placed Nick's tube on his desk then sat on my bed. The tube had a tag to help pull the lid off. I pulled the tag and seen some papers rolled up inside. Nick strolled into the room as I was looking and went under his desk for food. I looked at the time, 9 am. The papers included; the results from the second test, a new schedule for the year and information about my major.

Nick turned to me, "What's that?" his mouth was stuffed with food.

"Some results from the test."

Nick clumsily walked over to me, "Where is mine?"

"I put it on your desk."

Nick walked away and picked up the tube, he dropped it on the ground then picked it up. My major was something called ultrasomnology. According to the information, the study seemed scattered. It involved studying human sleep patterns along with dreaming and how sleep affects the body mentally and physically. My schedule included classes like; psychology, sleep science, neo-science and the list went on.

I looked in the tube again and noticed a paper wrapped around the side of the tube. I pulled it out, the title of the paper was, "results of the partner matching."

'Congratulation, as a result of your paper and blood test; you have been paired with your partner. Rosella Animous, is your partner. Your results came about from picking your close genetics compatible person; matched along with your personal matching questions. You and your partner are to report to the medical building room 417 at 4:06 Tuesday.'

"Hey I'm going to be a pharmacist. What did you get?"

"Ultrasomnologist?"

"What's that?"

"No idea I guess I'm going to be working with sleeping and dreaming or something."

"Seems like you got gypped. Being a pharmacist will be perfect!" Nick went into the bathroom. I looked back at the pattern results. Rosella Animous, no description, no picture, no comments nothing.

"Hey Nick who is your partner?"

"Not sure only looked at the major. I don't really care about a partner."

"Really? So what are you going to do about her?"

"Not sure, that's her problem."

"So you're going to be a male Mary?"

Nick was silent for a moment, "Well I will just tell her I don't want her. I already found the love of my life; and she takes my mind on a trip with every leaf."

Later that day after our performance at the Red Note we all sat down with Tim and talked about the test. "Well what questions did they have this year?" Tim had a presence about him few people had. Now he looked like a smooth picture perfect person. You still knew he was highly intelligent, this combination made him stand out more.

Bryan swallowed some steak, "one question on the moral part asked, 'if your friend needed help on a test what would you do?'"

Tim chuckled, "I had a question like that on mine. I said I would let him fail."

"Ha wow you jerk." Bryan gulped down some water.

"Well sorry if you didn't do the work to succeed, I'm not helping."

Nick's eyes were red, "We all need to keep ourselves alive now don't we."

Everyone but Tim felt awkward; Tim shook his head, "You better be careful. If I didn't know you I would think you were a barbarian. We only do things for the unity of us."

Nick had a look, "Then why wouldn't you help someone?"

"Well because they can't help the unity."

Jesse spoke, "But what if that person needed help to help themselves?"

Tim thought, "Well someone only helps themselves when the need is greater than what they want."

Bryan spoke, "but what if you don't show them more to life and they don't know what to want?"

Tim shrugged, "That's their problem. People need to find their own way and not follow down the path of a barbarian." There was an empty void in the air. Tim was now the oldest here but there was no replacement for Max.

"What Major did you guys get? I'm in Law class." Jesse waited for our responses.

Nick smiled almost empty minded, "I'm in pharmacy."

Bryan spoke with a straight face, "I'm in law class too."

Tim was curious, "You got into Law class? And you? You guys must have the same personalities on the inside for the test to give you that."

Bryan shrugged, "Who would have thought. What did you get into?" he pointed his cup in my direction.

"I guess I got put in ultrasomnology."

"What's that?"

Tim answered, "It's the study of sleep right?"

I nodded, "I guess I learn about sleep and how dreams and stuff affect the brain or something."

Jesse spoke, "That's something interesting. What kind of answers did you put on your personality test?"

"Not sure, I answered it normally."

Jesse looked over at the band playing, "well maybe you will like it."

"So what do you guys think about our partner results?" I waited for someone to respond.

Jesse spoke first, "I wish I knew who she was."

Tim spoke next, "Your generation isn't that close. My generation knows everyone. Maybe because we have been together for so long."

Bryan looked over at him, "So what do we do? Just wait till we see them when we report at the medical building?"

Tim shook his head, "no, I went out of my way to find my partner."

"How did you do that?"

Tim turned to me, "Well I knew her already and knew where to find her. If you guys want to meet up with your partner you should ask around."

Bryan pushed his empty plate; "I think I'm going to meet mine tomorrow."

Nick chuckled, "Some one's eager."

"Well might as well make sure I don't have a Mary."

Nick was playing with his cup, "I'm just going find out when I find out."

The next day Bryan, Jesse and I were standing by the football fields. "What time are you meeting her?" Jesse was waiting for Bryan's response.

"Well I asked around with a lot of people. It took a while to find someone who knew her and I guess it was her friend. Her friend said she would meet me here in an hour."

Jesse turned to me, "When are you meeting yours?"

"I heard people who want to meet their partners are all showing up either at the soccer field, music building or restaurant outside the English building."

"Why those places?"

"Not sure."

Jesse thought for a moment, "It's probably because they figure couples would think alike and go to the same place."

"Well then I guess I'm going to the music building."

"What are you doing?"

Jesse shrugged, "I guess I'll try to find her tomorrow."

Bryan stood up, "Well I'm going to head out. I'll tell you guys how it goes later."

Jesse turned to me, "You think the test would be accurate?"

"I'm not sure. I thought people would find their own way. Never thought you just needed to study all the factors about people then say you know what's best."

Later I was at the music building alone. All the rooms were decorated by genre. People who liked and took classical music in one room; everyone who liked pop music were in one room. Everyone who was coming seemed to be here by 7. I started bouncing around from room to room. Every room was playing music that genre round romantics. Everyone here seemed to find their partners fast and after an hour it looked like everyone found each other. It felt rather awkward because I was without my partner. People came up and talked to me, some asked me if I knew this person or that person and moved on. Only two girls walked up to me thinking I was their partner but we quickly found out we weren't. By the end of the night everyone was in one room under one genre with their partners. I just went home and figured I would go to the restaurant tomorrow.

The next day Jesse, Bryan and I were all together. Jesse was looking at the floor. "I'm surprised you're not with her now."

Bryan smiled, "Well we planned on seeing each other tonight."

"So you guys really connected then?"

"Yea, I didn't think it would be that perfect."

Bryan turned to me, "I think this might be one of the few things this place got right. You guys should keep hope."

"So she's everything you wanted?"

Bryan smiled at me, "Well so far. Her personality is just right. She's smart; she doesn't seem like a Mary, She's pretty. She's going to take classes in culinary. It's perfect."

I thought for a moment, "You are in Law class and she is in culinary. That seems like an interesting mix."

Bryan nodded; Jesse turned to Bryan, "How did you get into law class. You didn't seem to be into anything that would put you there before."

Bryan started confessing, "I want to finish what Max started."

Jesse and I looked at each other. Jesse turned back to Bryan, "What do you mean?"

"I've been thinking. Max wanted to change things. I think I know what he was going to do. If he got that job then he could slowly change laws. I'm going to try and do it."

"You want to do that?"

Bryan turned to me, "Yea, Max said we could achieve our dreams and my dream is to finish this. So far I already got into law class."

Jesse interrupted him, "But how? Did you do something funny?"

"No, I just answered the test the way Max would. It took me a long time, but I analyzed the questions and tried to pick out any answer that seemed like it would put me in Max's shoes."

"That's impressive, you're going to have to follow up with this or they will find out."

"Well I'm not worried. We are roommates anyway, so if I need a smart person I got one."

"Are you telling your partner?"

Bryan looked over at me thoughtfully, "I have to be careful with her. I mean if she's not on board right away, telling her could be risky."

Jesse spoke, "When it came to the partner questions how did you answer it?"

"I put down the opposite of Mary."

"Did you even put stuff down that you wanted?"

"Yea but I was careful so she wouldn't be out there."

Later that day I went to the restaurant hoping it would be better. It was crowded and they moved some tables around so people could dance. Each table was over populated. I sat down at a side table on the back wall of the building. In front of me was a dance floor and across that was a row of tables. I sat facing the crowd alone. I kept watching around the room hoping to see if I could find my partner. People were all trying to find their partners. You could almost smell the desperation in the air. Everyone was trying hard to impress whoever they thought their partners were. It was like no one bothered to ask each other for a name; if you asked I guess that would take the surprise out. But then again some people just seemed like they wanted to have fun; these few days would be the last few days before anyone had to make any commitments.

I sat alone waiting for my partner. I thought I would know her as soon as I seen her. An hour passed, I still couldn't find her. A group of girls came in and sat at an empty table across the dance floor from me. I didn't think much of it until one girl sat down facing my direction. She had a bright smile; her eyes were brown, her checks and forehead were round. A lot of the other girls around her just seemed to be plain compared to her. Her hair was dark and she let it hang with tight curls. She seemed to know everyone who passed by. Her skin was lighter and she stood out.

I thought for a moment, this could be her. I saw her look away from her friends and we caught eyes. For a moment I thought she blushed. I stood up and another girl walked in front of me. "Hey are you looking for your partner?"

I looked behind her at the table. The girl I was looking at seemed to awkwardly look away. A guy came up to her and she put out a smile. The guy reached out and they went to dance. I turned back to the girl in front of me. She was as tall as me with light brown hair. "Yea I'm looking for my partner."

"Hey me too." she seemed like she was trying hard to like a stranger. "So tell me about you."

"Me? Well I perform at the Red Note. I play guitar."

"Wow I play guitar too." I thought maybe this could be her. "So have you eaten yet?"

"No I haven't."

"Well I'll call over a waiter. You can sit here."

I sat back down with the girl. I called over someone to take our orders. I looked back at the table across the dance floor. The girl with the smile seemed upset and was walking away from the guy she danced with. She sat down and the guy tried to follow her. She got mad at him and he went away. When her friends came she smiled and acted like nothing happened.

The girl I was eating with called me, "This is my friend." Her friend was shorter then her with straight blond hair.

"It's nice to meet you."

The girl with light brown hair talked with me for a bit. Her friend with blond hair tried to talk to me and I tried to talk back. The girl with light brown hair got jealous and interrupted our conversation. The girls started talking between themselves and whispered. I overheard part of their conversation.

"Do you even know if it's him?"

"No but I think it's him."

"So then why are you flirting with mine?"

"I'm not."

"But you want to?"

"And if I do?"

"Well you know you will lose your guy."

"I known but I'm not flirting."

"Whatever."

We continued talking for a bit then the girl with blond hair awkwardly left. I got the girl with the brown hair's attention, "Why did she leave?"

"O you are such a flirt."

"What do you mean?"

"Please the way you looked at her. You are just like the last guy I thought was my partner."

"Is your name Rosella?" I looked quickly over at the table across the dance floor at the girl with the smile. She seen me with the girl with light brown hair then looked away. I turned back quickly.

"No, that's not my name." She got up and left.

I looked back over at the girl with the smile. She was watching me. A guy walked up to her and reached out to her. He pulled her to the dance. I sat back in my seat. After a while I decided to get up and found my way to a table with two girls at it. One had straight black hair and the other had curly hair. I thought maybe the girl with straight hair was my partner and started talking with her. She seemed shy at first then I noticed she just didn't seem she wanted to talk. Her friend with curly hair was talking to me and I figured, might as well check if she's it. The girl with straight hair stayed quiet while I and the girl with curly hair talked. After some time the girl with straight hair started getting jealous and eventually the girl with curly hair just stopped talking to me. It wasn't one of them so I moved on.

As I walked away I looked back quickly and when I turned back around I bumped into someone. The person was shorter than me. The face was the girl with the smile. I looked down at her and she was silent. "Hey sorry about that."

Her voice was nice and welcoming, "it's fine I wasn't watching where I was going. Are you looking for your partner too?"

I smiled, "Yes I am."

"Well any idea of who that might be?"

"Well I know the name of the person from the test so."

"O what's the first letter?"

"R"

"Rosella right?"

"Yea are you her?"

She had a bright smile, "That's me."

I struggled to find some words, "So, um, you know my name right?"

"Yes I do, it was in the partner stuff."

"So um."

She smiled, "You want to go for a walk?"

"Sure, where to?"

"I don't know let's just walk."

We went out of the building and headed down the street. I looked forward not knowing what to say. She turned to me, "so what class do you have?"

"I guess I've been put in something called ultrasomnology."

"What's that?"

"I don't really know. What about you?"

"I've been put in music classes."

"Really? I play guitar."

"Maybe you can help me. I want to be a singer but my voice isn't the best."

"Really? Sing, let's hear it."

"I'm horrible, other people say I'm good but I'm not."

"Well you're going to have to be a singer. So why not start?"

She shrugged, "Alright why not." She started singing beautify.

"Your voice is amazing."

"I hate my voice. I think it sounds horrible."

"Well then, do you work right now?"

"Yea I work as a chef at one of the restaurants here."

"At least one of us could cook."

She smiled, "I like food. So, what about you?"

"I'm a musician, that's my job."

"Wow, I'm surprised you haven't been put in music class. It would make sense."

"Yea, I'm not too sure about my test."

"What do you mean?"

"Ultrasomnology? Why do I have that for a class?"

"Well I'm not too sure about my classes either; but I can tell my partner test was right."

I smiled, "You think so?"

"Well so far my partner is nice and not like the other guys here."

"And what makes this different?"

"Well by now other guys would be asking about sex. A couple of my friends said their partners are already thinking about it. You haven't, that's probably a good record."

"O thank you. How many guys did you talk to tonight?"

She shrugged and bluntly said, "Two"

"Two?"

"Yup, two. If you're going to be my partner might as well be honest. I thought two other guys were my partner."

"It's what I thought someone else was mine too."

"Yea I saw."

"I thought it might have been you when I saw you but I wasn't sure."

"I thought you were too, but I just doubted it." It was getting late, she turned to me, "I'll meet you tomorrow at the music building at 10 am, unless you are busy."

"Tomorrow? No I'm free just a performance at the Red Note at seven. That would be fine." She hugged me and walked off.

The next day Bryan, Jesse and I were sitting on a bench by the football field. "Well she is amazing but one problem;

She's been trained to think civilly." Bryan had a semi-disappointed look.

Jesse started talking, "So now you have to hold your thought even at your own home."

"Yup, I have to be craftier each day."

"Are you ever going to tell her?"

Bryan looked at me, "Well if I can do it in a way she will understand and not turn me in then sure."

Jesse shifted the conversation, "How was meeting your partner?"

I looked at him, "She's nice. I'm planning on meeting her in an hour."

"Don't forget we have to play at the Red Note."

"We are meeting before that and I'm probably going to invite her."

Bryan smiled, "I invited my partner, and we can all sit at the same table with Tim's partner. Of course someone hasn't found his yet."

We all looked at Jesse, "Well people in law class are getting there early so I'm going to get a jump on things. Are you coming?" Jesse shrugged and stood up.

Later I met up with Rosella at the music building. There was a mini festive going on there to welcome the new freshmen. Rosella came over to me and gave me a large hug. "Hey how are you?"

I smiled, "Fine, later today do you want to go to the Red Note?"

"The Red Note? That fancy place? Is this your first time playing there?"

"No, I and my band perform there along with the comedian Tim."

"Sorry I don't know who that is."

"I guess you wouldn't really know unless you go to the Red Note often."

"Yea, it's always hard to get in there unless you have money. I never bothered trying."

"Why not? It's a nice place."

"It's just not the place for me. I don't think I would belong there."

"I thought you want to be a singer? You could belong as a singer."

"It was a thought, how would you get a place for me in the Red Note?"

"I can bring whoever I want because my band is a higher ranked band and stuff."

"O so the rich give other privileges to the rich."

"What do you mean?"

"Just when you're higher up you get some things different then everyone else."

"Well I mean getting ahead in life just depends on what you do. Anyone can get ahead; the better you treat your work the better they perform for you."

She thought for a moment, "Then what about everyone else?"

I shrugged, "Well they can't help everyone in the world. You can only help those who want to help themselves."

She grabbed my hand, "You are smart aren't you?"

"Sure I guess."

"That's good, what do you think leaving this place will be like?"

"I had a friend who was a senior. He said before he left that he was getting a house."

"O what happened to him? He graduated right?"

I thought for a moment, "I don't know. He went away."

"Well that sounds nice, a place away from here."

"You don't like it here?"

"You do?"

"No."

"Well I don't. I hate it here. None of the stuff we learn I'm going to use."

"You could use whatever singing you learn."

"I guess."

"The music class you were put in should help."

"I guess, I just want to be free and live without having all these teachers hovering around you."

"Wow, so you must not like this system."

"Nope."

"And you don't like the laws?"

"I don't even know anything; I don't have to know them."

"You're not afraid of sounding like a barbarian?"

"I'm not sure about all that stuff. We can't be individuals but we have our own classes? We can listen to our own music? We like our own foods? Obviously we are all barbarians."

"You know I haven't met many people like you."

"What you don't like it? If not I don't know what to say; I am what I am." She looked away.

"No, you are fine. I'm actually happy because we have something in common. The last person I met like us was that senior I told you about."

She hugged me, "You're comfortable."

"That's random."

"I guess, I'm weird sometimes."

Later that day, Jesse, Bryan, Tim, Bryan and Tim's partner, Rosella and I were all together at the Red Note. We all walked our partner in and sat them down at the same table, then went to go perform. It went like a typical night; we played a song while Tim was in the spotlight. Tim first played a song then went into a comedic act. During Tim's act we would stop playing until he made a joke and at the right time, we would play sound effects and make everything sound welcoming. Whenever Tim stopped talking, he normally gave people time to laugh so we would play something to help the mood. The whole time I was looking over at the table where Rosella was; then looked away to pay attention to when I had to play.

She smiled and turned red when I looked over. She didn't seem to pay attention to Tim's jokes and she didn't say much to Tim or Bryan's partners. When the show was done the guys and I slipped off stage by going behind the curtains then down to our table. Rosella grabbed my hand as soon as I sat down, "You were really good tonight." She smiled as she spoke.

Tim turned to Bryan, "well sounds like you guys are happy. What about you too?" he spoke to Rosella and I.

"We are doing well."

"That's good; don't forget to get your recommended time together."

Rosella seemed curious, "Recommended time?"

"Yea, partners should spend a recommended time together. Experiments and studies have shown that people who spend the recommended time together have better relationships. All of you might want to look into it."

Bryan got Tim's attention, "So do you know why we have to report to the medical building later next week?"

I turned to Bryan, "We have to report there in a few days."

Tim thought for a moment, "I think it's just for a medical checkup and to help register for an official partnership and paper work. Everyone goes through it once. I don't remember it that well. It wasn't a big deal."

Tim's partner spoke, "Yea it's not much of a big deal. I forgot we even did that."

I turned to Rosella, "You should have seen Max singing he was really good."

Bryan shook his head, "One of a kind, without his singing we probably wouldn't have gotten our start."

Rosella looked at him, "Why? You guys are great."

Jesse started speaking, "Most people don't care about instrumentals. Some people feel like if there isn't a singer then it's not even good music."

"Well all these people were listening when you played your song tonight."

Tim answered, "That's because here you come to eat and listen to music. It's a different audience than your average person listening to pop; plus they were waiting for my act."

Bryan turned to Tim, "what are we going to do without you; first Max, now you. We need something special to make us standout more."

Tim shrugged, "you guys will still have a job here. Just come out with a new instrumental every month or so."

Bryan leaned back, "That's not enough."

Tim took a sip of some water, "Then find a new singer."

Jesse smiled, "And where are we going to find one?"

I turned to Rosella, "She can sing pretty well."

She looked at me surprised, "What?"

Tim smiled, "can you?"

"I can."

Bryan started questioning her, "Do you have any musical experience?"

"Well I've sang before, not professionally like you guys; and I'm going into music class now."

Jesse jumped the gun, "Can you sing a little for us now?"

Rosella gave me a look, "I'm not sure."

Tim shrugged, "Well you could easily fill in for me when I leave; and we can give you time to practice. I'm pretty sure you would be the one of the first female performers to hold a spot light at the Red Note in a while."

Bryan started speaking, "We still need her to sing for us."

We all looked at her. Rosella just let everything go, "Why not." She started singing; everyone at the table was amazed. Her voice was perfectly hitting notes, she sang with passion and confidence. Some people at the tables around us stopped to listen to her. She stopped singing when she noticed she was getting attention. We all clapped.

Tim smiled, "Well, I'm sure you will fit in well with us."

When everything was over I walked Rosella to her home. Right when we left the Red Note, she turned to me with a half smile, "I can't believe you just did that."

I smiled, "What?"

"You didn't have to throw me out there like that."

"You sing amazingly and we have time before you would go on. I mean if you don't want to its fine."

She looked at the sky then at the floor, "Well I guess. We will see how practice goes."

The time came for me and Rosella to report to the medical building. I met her before we went and we walked over together. We walked into the room we were assigned. There was a man behind a desk with two chairs opened for us. "Come in, please." The man was the head of the health department. "Take a seat please." We walked over and sat down in the seats. "So have you two met before?"

I answered first, "Yes we have."

"Before the test or after the test?"

Rosella answered, "After."

The head of department started writing, "That's nice, you two are happy?"

"Yes we are." We spoke almost in unison.

"Well, seems you two are happy. Now please keep in mind the rest of your career here at this school will help determine where you two will live. You two will both contribute factors to how your home will be determined. Now on to the important matter. I know this is a long-term effect and it may sound like a large step. All members of society are required to undergo a sterilization process to help regulate the birth and rate of our population. You both must go through this process. Some people are given special permission to skip this process so long as their genes are suitable for future generations. In this group, people who have suitable genes may have the option to submit recourses for child growing. Others who are suitable may be required to submit their recourses if their genes are exceptional. By Law only one partner in a partnership are allowed to skip the sterilization process if both qualify with ideal genes. Now with that said, you both qualify. If you two decided that one of you would submit resources then that person must report once a month to a medical center to submit your recourses. Now you two must make a decision." The room was silent for a moment.

I looked over at Rosella and she looked at me. She turned to the department head, "What happens during the sterilization process?"

The department head spoke as if he rehearsed these lines, "The person under sterilization will take a pill every morning for 30 days. The person is required to take them and must give a urine sample each afternoon to their assigned medical center to provide proof they followed instructions. The process is known to be painful and reports come in with great discomfort. The other option is to undergo surgery. The person must have the money before hand. Pain is reported to only last the week after surgery; the cost is high. 10,000 drops."

I turned to Rosella and looked at the department heads, "Why do we have to go under this process?"

The department head leaned back, "We have to regulate the population. It's the only responsible and moral way to do so under the law.

Rosella spoke, "If we submit the resources will we ever see the children?"

The department spoke emotionless, "Have you seen your biological donors? That won't change much. If you see them you will never know it's them.

"We have parents?"

The department head spoke carefully, "'parents' would be the slang version of biological donors; but that is as far as it goes. You are just biologically similar."

"Why don't we ever meet them?"

"I told you, you can but you just won't know it's them."

"Could we see them when we leave this place?"

"Mrs. Rosella, let me explain. In the time when barbarianism was rampant spread, a couple million years ago; people lived together in something known as a family. You may use this as slang for people who are close. In these times it meant that a person's offspring were subject to their male and female donors; a mother and a father. These mothers and fathers taught their own offspring and everyone grew up learning barbaric ways. People had no order or structure, no law of the civilized man. As you learn in school and the virtual adolescents' trainer; the people who helped start the movement for a civil humanity were trying to change what a 'family' meant. After some time the family had to go all together. The family was going against the civil law. Fathers and mothers taught barbarism, people were corrupt; children didn't always have the greatest of opportunities, some lived in rich families while others lived in poor. Some had abusive parents while others had better. Not anymore, now the law changed that. Everyone is stripped from this burden, everyone is the same, and everyone is now equal. Of course without a mother and a father coming together in a partnership; the population would drop. So we found a way to keep the population striving while still saving humanity from barbaric ideas. That is why we need you two to make a choice. You two are doing a higher duty for your people. The only way it would be required for both partners to donate would be if we did not have a correct number of people giving resources. Of course resource submission is only allowed for ten years after you have found your partner; purely for quality reasons."

"So when do we need to make a choice?"

The head of the department looked at me; "I can give you until the end of the day." he reached into his desk, "Maybe this could help you decide." He handed us a pamphlet.

The next school year started; new freshmen had already been shipped in by bus. It felt strange with all the new people trying to adjust to the changes on campus. Some thought they were in charge and got put in their place rather quickly. Others seemed insecure and nervous to be on their own without the virtual teacher.

We started practicing with Rosella; she started singing some of Max's song to start. Our schedules started to feel like a rut and everything started up just like last year. We continued to have blood drawings every gym class. It was so common I forgot to mention it when it happened. It was almost like walking into a room and turning on a light bulb.

My first class for ultrasomnology was in a smaller hallway in one of the science buildings. The class was on the study itself, which over lapped with other studies; which took me to a class on the brain, then a class on the science of dreaming, then another class in the study. The room I was in for my first class was small; it only had ten people. When I entered the room there was one professor and six other students.

"Welcome, come in. everyone is in the class so we will start." The man was bold with a long goatee. He had on a blue vest and white dress up shirt with a dark red tie. He turned to an old school chalk board and picked up some white rock then started writing his name, "Mr. Quizim, q, u, i, z, i, m." he turned to us all, "now notice I used a chalk board. Why? Because I am an old soul and this is an old study. The study talks about the deep things in rooted in human nature. The consciousness, human thought, how we understand things, why do we act the way we do, what governs our actions and ultimately; how do we dream." He walked around the room, "now a dream you may say. Why study them? In the old ages, people believed dreams were desires of the heart and were manifestations of what we wanted outside of others who witness what we do. Here we will look at it; dreams, goals, hope, and plans. In this class you need to define what this thing is. For us we need to define a dream. Is a dream simply an image that appears when you close your eyes? What about a daydream? Is a dream a hope or a goal? What is a dream?"

He asked around the room; he called one person, then another and another. We gave our own idea of what a dream was and after the first two people it seemed we came back to the same basic ideas. "You all have ideas, which is good, but you need to know what is correct." He turned to the board, "lesson one; a dream is a combination of the following: hope, faith and ideas. The combinations of these make up a 'dream'." He stopped writing on the board, "Ok now you think you know what a dream is, you think you know all these words." He paused for a moment, "you are wrong, in this class you need to define and make clear what exactly it is that we are talking about. These things are things that we can't yet to directly observe, things that aren't easily tested. It's not something you can hold in your hand. For this reason you need to be clear as to what you're talking about."

    He turned back to the board, "The easiest one is an idea, you all know what this is. You know the light bulb in your head. I want to invent this idea, I think things should be run this way; I have a story I want to write this way. This is so hard to define because we are so familiar with it; but here we go. A thought or conception, that potentially or actually exists in the mind as a product of mental activity. This is one way to define an idea." He wrote all this down on one part of the board. "The next element is hope, as a noun: a feeling of expectation and desire for a certain thing to happen; as a verb: the want of something to happen or to be the case. This is one way to define it."

    He started on the last section on the board, "now for faith: faith is the substance of things hoped for, the evidence of things not seen. Simply put faith is as if what you hoped exists, even though you don't see evidence of It." He turned to us, "See it all starts with an idea, you have an image in your mind. So you have another idea to paint it. You have a hope to see it in reality. From there you start painting with hope and it will be done. You have faith as you paint it, your idea becomes reality, it becomes real, it become the image of your mind in physical reality before it's done. So this is a dream; dreams manifest in different ways. For some people their sub-conscience creates this in their sleep. For others it is a goal. Yet others it's just that; a dream."

    He looked around at us, "dreams are both good and bad. See some dreams are civilized like the dreams we have to bring order to man to stop barbarianism. Other dreams are deadly, like doing illegal activities. Some of you will leave this campus with a degree in ultrasomnology and go onto great things; some do. ultrasomnology to help us understand how these dreams effect us; what dreams take someone from simply a Joe to a leader? What barbaric dreams do you need to turn to a rebel in hiding or a rebellion starter? Do two people need the same dream to have the same effect? Does a dream affect everyone differently? If we gave someone a dream, will their life change? Part of your study will take you to better understand the brain to help see if you can predict these things. To see if you can find what it takes to change the course of some one's life forever."

At lunch Rosella and I met up at a restaurant. We sat at a table looking over the menu. "So what do you think about that?"

She shrugged and held my hand, "Sounds like an interesting class."

I chuckled, "That's it?"

"What?"

"Well sounds interesting. You could probably use this to help with that seniors' dream you told me about."

"You're talking about Max?"

"Yea, that's his name."

"Maybe, how's music going?"

"Not bad so far, but I'm not sure if I can do this."

"Why not?"

"Because some of the people in there have amazing skill. I can't compete with that."

"Sure you can, you just have to give it some time. I'll help you if you need me."

"Thanks but I don't know, it's frustrating so far. They expect you to know what a tonic is and how to do inversions and stuff."

"I know that stuff."

"I don't know, it's all kind of hard. I think I'm just going to try to get another class."

I remembered what Max said, "No you shouldn't."

"But I will never be like those other people. I'm not going to be successful."

"Can I tell you something?"

She looked at me with watering eyes, "What?"

"I've noticed something, Max started to show me this but I didn't quite get it until we played at the Red Note. You don't have to be professional to be successful. You don't have to have the best grades or anything; you don't have to be educated, you don't have to have money. You can do what you want; like our band, none of us were in music school. We had little background in music. Most of what we know we learned from Max, each other or on our own. Frankly we only played in smaller restaurants around and on the streets we didn't have much to say we would be successful. We just went and talked with teachers and practiced ourselves. Now we are playing and competing with 'professionals', which we shouldn't be doing. It doesn't fit what people said you have to do. After seeing some people coming out of music school I noticed there are two kinds of 'professionals.' 1.) The people who everyone becomes where they learn to copy other work and play by the rules and don't do anything out of the ordinary.2.) The other professionals are the ones we think about. The people who make new things and make new rules. They don't have to be like anyone else, they are themselves. Another thing I noticed is we don't remember the first kind but we remember the second kind. Those who are successful are people who put in work and have the desire to be great. Almost everyone is ok with settling, while others strive for greatness."

She seemed like she was thinking, "You think I can be one of them?"

"One of whom?"

"The greats."

"Well if you want to be, yes; and I will be right by your side the whole time to hold you up when you need it."

Rosella smiled and held me close.

After we had lunch I walked Rosella to her next class. We happened to pass by the green house. Nick was with a girl under a tree behind some bushes. Nick's eyes were red and he seemed completely relaxed. The girl was relaxed lying on his shoulder. She had long hair and dressed like a nature girl.

"Isn't that your bass player?"

"It is?" we walked over to him, "Hey Nick?"

Nick looked up in a daze, "Is that you? O hey man. How are things?"

"Ok what are you doing here?"

"O, I'm just with my partner. She knows some powerful plants. You want to try some?"

The girl slapped him, "Do you know how hard it is to get these leaves? You don't just give them away to anyone."

I spoke to Nick, "So you just drug up on the streets?"

"Yea, pretty much."

"What if you get caught?"

"No one will catch us. If you don't want to chill, then go. I'll be at the next performance."

"Aren't you going to class?"

"Class? My teacher was so impressed I knew so much about medicine he said he doesn't mind if I'm there or not unless my grade suffers"

Rosella pulled my arm, "We are going to be late." We moved on. Nick sat up, "If you need a chew let me know."

When we were far enough Rosella turned to me, "What's with him, didn't you say Max took his punishment?"

"Yea he did."

"Do you think Max knew he would waste his life?"

"I'm not sure."

"So why did Max do it?"

"So we had a chance."

Over the next few months, changes happened at the Red Note. Rosella started to perform. At first the manager didn't want her because we already had a reputation; but he let her try it out. We took a two-hour slot where we would play with her singing for one hour; then Tim's act for one hour. One hour was generally one group of people and the next hour was another. After Rosella preformed, more people started coming to the Red Note to see us. We even had more people who wanted to perform. Many of the new people coming in were girls who Rosella inspired to sing.

The new group of freshmen that came in all wanted to have fun and often held parties every weekend. A lot of the new performers came to the Red Note and it soon became their tradition to have a get together every Friday, after eight.

This Friday the band finished performing and we sat in the audience to eat. Rosella was next to me, Tim next to his partner, Bryan with his and Jesse was alone. "I'm not surprised because you're quiet. But you're not shy."

Jesse shrugged, "she just isn't a social person. I mean I guess the test matched me with someone like me. She just keeps saying she's too shy to see you guys."

A freshman wearing a dark red suit walked up to the table with a girl in a white dress. The freshman had spiky hair. "Hello guys." We all turned and waved. "I am hosting a get together tonight and was wondering if you guys would come." We all looked at each other. The same thought went through our heads, 'hanging around little kids.' The guy started begging, "It would be fun, only people from the Red Note are coming, maybe a few others." No one responded, "It would be an honor to have you all, everyone has been talking about having Mrs. Animous and Mr. Tim at a get together. There will be tons of food." we all looked at our plates.

We all looked around and shrugged. Tim answered, "Ok we will go."

The guy smiled, "Excellent, it's from 8:30 to 10; at the music building, in the room with the dancing floor."

Tim spoke, "It must cost some money to rent the ball room."

"Well we wanted a room large enough for people to socialize but still have a stage for performers."

"Who's performing?"

"I have some people from the Red Note; I mean unless you would like to perform?"

Tim smiled, "We will see what happens."

The freshman looked around, "Where is your bass player?"

Bryan looked, "he probably slipped out after the performance."

"Will he come?"

Jesse answered, "No promises."

The freshman smiled; "Well thank you for your time." he walked off jittery.

Bryan turned to Tim, "Are we really going?"

Tim smiled, "Why not, if you don't want to you don't have too. But might as well support our fellow Red Note performers right?"

Later that night we all walked down to the music building together. It was Tim and his partner, then Rosella holding my hand, then Bryan and his partner and then Jesse walking in alone. As we walked into the building people were shocked to see us. They were all freshmen; every one of them tried to come up to us and asked for a picture and autograph. I turned to Rosella, "They don't know we all live in the same school right?"

Rosella smiled, "Don't question it, they are happy."

We walked down a hallway and stopped at the door to the room. Two bouncers were blocking the door. Tim walked up to them. "We are here." the bouncers stepped aside and opened the doors. As we walked in everything stopped and everyone noticed us. The freshmen that invited us came over and walked us to our seats. Everyone tried to go back to their conversations but all the freshmen wanted to talk to us. Some of them didn't belong to the Red Note but came because they had a reputation among the rest of the freshmen making them popular. Talking with one kid he told me how he set a record in the gym this year, another kid was so social everyone knew him.

We were all sitting down as people came up one by one to talk to us. Rosella had a ton of girls surrounding her seat asking questions. Finally one girl got the idea to have her sing on stage. Rosella smiled, "thanks but I don't think I will tonight. I already performed." Some of the girls kept asking and eventually everyone wanted to hear her in the room when they heard the girls asking. The singer in the band performing stopped and even invited Rosella. She finally stood up, "Alright, but he has to play guitar with me." Rosella picked me off my feet and hugged me. We walked up and the band cleared the stage for us. The guitarist on stage handed me his guitar and a stool.

    I heard him whisper, "Can you autograph this for me when you're done." Everyone was off the stage, it was just Rosella and I. She was standing next to a microphone stand. A light shinned around the two of us. Rosella smiled at me. I started strumming her favorite song and she joined in shortly after. At first the room was full with the sound of Rosella and me but then slowly everyone started singing along.

Adult hood

"As you can see, behavior is deeply affected by how the brain is wired. If you have your five senses stimulated, your brain will create chemical pathways entrapping that moment or even idea. Now with that said, this is risky. If a dream or bad teaching or bad image gets implanted in your brain, how do we un-wire it? We only know it's there, but how can we change that. Is a person unchangeable? This class is where you can usher in a new future. We simply know bad wiring can be reinforced casing the response to these wires to be stronger. How do I say that? Look at the new freshmen this year." Everyone in the room chuckled, "Something went wrong with their virtual simulation. They aren't like us. The sophomores that joined us last year were bad, but these guys are worse. Hopefully they don't keep coming like this." The bell rang. "You are all dismissed; Don't forget your essays next week."

It's a new year. Tim walked the stage before the break. He was moved on to some kind of science engineering job. What that meant, I don't know, but I was told it is a very high role with lots of government projects. The new freshmen who came in are not like anyone we seen in the past. They collectively have an average of 11 percent error. Most generations have no more than 4 percent error all together. I heard their best student has a 6 percent error. Either way I thought it wasn't any of my business.

Last year after Tim, Bryan, Jesse Rosella and I went to that one gathering we never went to another one again; even if someone from the Red Note hosted it. We didn't like getting stormed by the freshmen. Whatever happened to them in the virtual world really made a cultural difference between them and the juniors and seniors. There's just something different about them. Nick on the other hand started going every time there was a party or celebration of any kind. He turned into some kind of party animal.

Something kind of funny about the freshmen this year was most of them was really interested in chemistry. New laws were passed by the department head of health banning a lot of products used by the freshmen. Before we used to have different sodas and different candies but now they are illegal and the greenhouse was almost shut down three times. There's a ban on 30 percent of the plants grown in the past.

Now it's obvious many of the freshmen were taking illegal plants and making illegal substances. But the school could never prove it. But it was clear many of them were. Many places were band and staff were stationed basically anywhere a person could be alone. Now so many places were discovered with illegal plants almost everyone in the green house was suspected of crime. Funny thing was most of the people growing were everyday students, not members of the green house.

Many of the parties and gathering were basically formed for chewing plants and people showing off trying to get their reputation. It was all the freshmen and sophomore, and Nick who they all loved. I almost never saw Nick except when we played at the Red Note and when I was getting ready to leave for class. Several times he tried walking in the room with a smell that could get both of us in trouble. I forced him out every time. Other then that the only times I saw him was when he was with his partner using some plants or surrounded by freshmen being adored.

Rosella came to us at the right time; since Tim left she took over and people loved seeing her perform. Every night people would line up just to hear her voice. When the show was over we usually sat at a back table, just us.

After class today I planned on meeting Rosella by one of the football fields. We were both sitting on a bench talking. She had her head on my shoulder, "Well I'm not sure what to think of that. Your classes seem like they question whether or not we are even human. You guys might as well find out if we have any free will while you're at it."

"One guy next to me believes he found that answer."

"O really? And what was his big idea?"

Some freshmen walked up to us, "Can I have your autograph?"

Rosella looked up, "Sorry I'm busy right now, maybe later." She turned to me, "What was his idea?"

I tried to bring the memory of what he said back; "He said, 'our brains are just made up of chemical pathways. Since chemicals can be calculated and follow predictable patterns, there is no way of changing a person. Once the chemical pathways are created there is no going back and a person will always react the same way. These chemical pathways just need something to start their formation.' It was something like that."

Rosella was silent for a moment, "I don't see it. What if a new pathway was created over the old one? Or what if two memories contradicted each other?"

"That's a good point." I sat there amazed at her genius. She just thought of a key to the puzzle some of us studying would have taken years to find. I noticed she started to stare at me. "What are you thinking?"

She spoke bluntly, "Your hair is always messy and undone. But I love it."

I smiled, "You probably made the most important discovery in my studies history and you just move on so quickly."

She closed her eyes, "I have something more important in front of me."

Bryan and Jesse came over, "Ok, love time is over." Bryan came between us and forced himself between us. Jesse started speaking, "You won't believe this but I found out what happened."

"What do you mean?"

"I found out why the freshmen are so out of hand this year." Bryan stood up and walked next to Jesse.

I was interested to see what happened, "What?"

Jesse started explaining, "It seems they tried to start a new curriculum for the virtual simulation and something went wrong two generations ago. Now they are just seeing the results of the change and they tried to fix it last year but it seems things are just getting worse."

"Wow, they actually got something wrong for once?"

"From what I found, they tried to have a curriculum that would give people more personality."

I chuckled, "It seems like they are all clones of each other now."

"Yea, they did something and it just made the generation to come less intelligent. I seen a clip of some of the virtual simulations running and they made everything seemed more childish. I guess it stunned their brain development and now took away their filters."

Bryan chuckled, "so in other words they became like Nick."

Jesse spoke, "What's he been up to lately?"

"He's nuts. Every time there's a party he's there. I'm surprised though, he uses so many plants and yet they haven't found out about him."

Jesse continued, "They are onto him, I heard some teacher's talking about him using plants but I didn't think it was true."

"We should do something about this." everyone looked at me.

Bryan said, "And what do you think we should do?"

"I don't know but if he gets caught this will look bad on us."

Jesse nodded and Rosella said, "How?"

Bryan spoke, "our group was suspected of illegal plants before. If another person turns up for the same thing, that's problem."

Rosella grabbed my hand, "So let's go talk to him, where can we find him?" None of us knew, "you said he's always at these parties so let's go looking for him. When's the next one?"

Jesse and Bryan looked at each other. Bryan spoke, "I know today there's supposed to be a big one at the soccer fields. Some freshmen were keeping it quiet."

Rosella was surprised, "Really? The school is allowing this?"

Jesse shook his head, "No this is just supposed to be a really big one though. I heard they planned on bringing out tents and lots of food. It's like the fourth time they did this."

Bryan knotted, "They have been doing a lot of them out in the open. Just really close to curfew."

Rosella was surprised, "Why haven't I heard about this?"

Bryan chuckled, "Because they are freshmen and sophomores; and the school doesn't want the word to spread anyway. They keep having parties in new places and only use the same place when the school stops guarding the old places."

Later we met up at the soccer field. It was Rosella, Bryan's partner and I. Bryan brought her alone because she didn't believe the reason why he was coming. Instead she got the idea he was going to cheat. We didn't know why, but Jesse wasn't here and we waited ten minutes then decided to go without him. The soccer field had rough tents set up and decorations thrown up crudely. Everything looked like it was last minute and was even made of random stuff. It was like if they needed to leave quickly it wouldn't matter because they could leave the plastic bags they used to make tents. They even hung Christmas lights from tent to tent because they couldn't turn on the field's light.

Somehow they managed to get tons of chairs and stacked them in places for people to come and take. Looking at everything I just knew no one was planning on cleaning up. Everything was packed with little kids running around. Rosella was close behind me while I pushed through the crowd. We tried looking around for Nick but couldn't find him. Rosella pulled me aside from the crowd, "Maybe he's not here."

"I don't know I mean what are the odds, he doesn't come to the one party we are trying to find him at."

I looked around, "Where's Bryan?"

Rosella looked, "I don't know, let's go get him."

"You mean I find him in that crowd?"

"Well I mean how else we should find him."

"Let's try to get out of this mess first." Rosella followed me as we tried moving our way off the soccer field.

As we moved through the crowd one of the freshmen went over and touched Rosella. His eyes were red. Rosella turned and slapped the guy across the face, "Why are you touching me?"

The guy backed up, "I just wanted to have some fun; what's wrong with you?"

Rosella turned, "Can't you see I'm taken?" Some of the people stopped and watched Rosella talking to the guy. The guy tried to reach for Rosella again, "that's ok with me girl." Rosella pushed his hand and got ready to punch him. I grabbed her arm and pulled her around to a tent.

Rosella looked away at the ground. I put my arms around her, "It's ok. Look at me." she looked up at me with her eyes angry and watering, "It's fine."

"If you weren't here I would have punched him in the throat." She hugged me back.

Two freshmen walked by and seen us, "I heard he's coming today."

"You sure?"

"Yes, he's in the bitter root drinking contest."

I called one of them, "Who are you talking about?"

One of the kids turned, "Animal Nick." They went off ignoring us for not knowing.

Rosella looked at me, "Animal Nick? What kind of name is that?"

"I don't know but that probably means he is here after all."

"Let's go get him." Rosella grabbed my hand and started walking, "Let's find Bryan first." We finally made our way off the soccer field and headed over to the bleachers off to the side. We went up to the top of the bleacher's and tried to see if we could get a good idea of the area. Over in the middle of the field was an open area with tables and crates lined up. Rosella was scouting out everything. I heard two voices and turned around for a moment and she looked under a tree behind the bleachers.

"No, we shouldn't be happy living like this. Life can be different."

"If life was different everything would be barbaric. People would be out of control."

I looked down to see Bryan and his partner talking, "Look at this, people are out of control now. We are simply covering up flaws that are just in human nature."

"No what we have are barbarians living in our society."

"No it's human nature, we aren't perfect. We have flaws, we make errors."

His partner backed up; "Well if we make errors then I guess the humans grading our test made a large one." she started walking off.

"Where are you going?"

"I will die before I support any barbarian."

Bryan stood heartbroken. Rosella and I went over to him, "Are you ok?"

Bryan looked at me trying to be strong, "It's fine, and I'm fine. I know she just doesn't understand what Max did for us."

"What are you going to do now?"

Bryan closed his eyes, "When she's ready I will be here. But in either way I have to keep going."

Rosella spoke, "Here?"

"I'm still going to fix the system. Max may not have, but I will do it."

"Well lets go, I know where Nick will be." we followed Rosella to an open space with tables. We couldn't get close because there was a crowd of people blocking everything making a circle. We could only see over the heads of these kids. On the fields each table had hundreds of cups with brown liquid in them. On the side of each table were freshmen all spaced out waiting. Nick was at one table; his had cups of liquid stacked strategically.

A voice called out of a megaphone, "it's time for the bitter root juice contest! First to drink the most in five minutes and hold it down wins!"

I turned to Bryan, "What's bitter root juice?"

"It's an illegal mix of several different plants squeezed to their pups. Individually they are completely legal to have and are even grown in the green house often. When combined they become mind altering to the user. It was band this year"

"How?"

"I don't know exactly. I think they change together by a chemical reaction."

Everyone started cheering. I looked up and the freshmen in the contest were gulping down cup after cup. Rosella pulled my arm, "Why are we waiting here, let's go get him."

Bryan turned, "You mean go in front of this mess?"

"Well why not? We have him now and who knows for how long?"

Bryan sighed, "I don't know if that's a good idea."

Rosella shrugged, "I'm going now. You can wait if you want too."

Rosella pushed through the people and came out into the open area. People started cheering for her as if she was going to join in the contest. Rosella went up to Nick; he continues gulping down liquid ignoring her. Rosella started saying something but I couldn't tell because people started screaming louder. Nick gave a quick response and actually stopped drinking for a moment to yell out something then went right back. Rosella looked angry and stepped closer with her fist tight. The loud screaming seemed to feel like it was louder and coming closer too. Nick jumped on the table and splashed a cup in Rosella's face. I started pushing through the crowd with Bryan somewhere behind me. Rosella stood for a moment looking at the juice dripping off her body. I tried running to her but the crowd started running from the left to the right in front of me. People pushed and bumped their way passed me. Slowly I was blocked and closed into a sea of people. I saw a table fly over every one's head with juice flying everywhere.

    A rather large husky freshman slammed into me and kept running. People ran over me and feet went all around my head. I tried curling into a ball to protect myself; a few people tripped over me and then picked themselves up. The crowd started to clear and I saw a kid getting tackled by a school emergency guard. I lifted myself up to look over the guard and kid on the ground. Rosella was on the floor; her leg looked like it was part of the table lying on the ground. My heart raced as I blinked and seen hundreds of red drops splattered across the table. I started running; still light headed from being trampled and getting hit on the head a few times. Before I was even close to her three guards were over her and a large body tackled me to the ground. My head jerked sideways; I felt the rough turf give me a rug burn as I blinked.

    The next moment I woke up in a chair; my face was on a cold metal table. I picked up my head still light headed to see the face of the head of the health department sitting in a chair with the men in black behind him. There was a white blinding light shining on the ceiling over the department head. He said my name, "You have been found guilty of; barbaric conduct, aiding and partaking in illegal action, possession and concealing of illegal plants and false witness under previous investigation." One of the men in black made his way over to me and placed a paper in front of me then walked back. As I looked at the paper he continued on, "You have been found guilty on all charges and your sentence will be executed at the close of this meeting."

"I did nothing wrong. When did this happen?" as I spoke I felt a pain in my head and the lights were giving me an even larger pain.

"We had all the witness we needed all to agree that you were partaking in an illegal event on the soccer field. Your band was investigated for illegal plants before. You all have been found at this event with illegal plants and some of you were found under the influence. A council of law students have reviewed the event and made their final conclusion."

"What happen to Rosella?"

"I'm sorry this is not of your concern; you two have lost partnership and are no longer recognized as under any legal bond under civil law."

"I didn't do anything wrong. Doesn't the law allow me to give a testimony?"

The head of the department was motionless, "This is only given to citizens. Barbarians are not citizens. You have lost your citizenship." My mind started to race at what this meant. "You will be transported to your barbaric land under the civil terms and conditions of war criminals. Now with this, we are done. I have explained everything I am legally bonded to and I no longer have any obligations to make contact with you." he stood up and started walking off.

"You can't just do this. I'm human too!" my head started feeling lighter. Some of the men in black walked over to me, "I deserve a chance." The men in black started reaching for me "Don't touch me!" I pushed back as I struggled for my life. "You must check the law. I am innocent." I fell on the floor and they grabbed my arms and lifted me. "You can't do this! You can't!" I struggled as they dragged me across the floor. I continued to struggle; one of the men in black pressed some metal object to my ribs. "Leave me alone! You cant-" I felt a pain spark into my ribs and my body started to go into shock. My limbs fell asleep as my head dangled. My eyelids opened and closed as my head bobbled around. One moment I got a glimpse of the hallway; the next moment was darkness, the next we were in an elevator, the next darkness. The next moment we passed by a room with Bryan struggling, the next darkness. The next moment we were outside, the next darkness. The next moment I saw Bryan struggling to carry me with the sound of rockets, then darkness.

I opened my eyes again and this time I could move my body. I was leaning up against a tree Bryan was against another tree holding his legs with his head down. I took a deep breath and sat in silently for a moment. A summer breeze whistled across my skin. I took another breath. Everything felt so free; the leaves twirled in the branches, sticks fell under the simply law of gravity but landed wherever it wanted. The sunlight pushed through the trees wherever it could fit.

I lifted myself up and smelt the air, "Bryan." he lifted his head with disappointment running down his face, "what happened?"

He wiped his tears, "Well what do you remember?"

"Rosella was talking to Nick. A crowd trampled me. Someone hit me; I was in a room. They questioned me and now we are here."

Bryan sighed, "Well the legal process for finding a barbarian in civil land states that; the barbarian found must be educated on their wrong doing then transported. Out here soldiers are sent to fight barbarians. The only reason they didn't kill us is because it's barbaric for crime to happen in a city; and not give any organism a chance at life if able too."

"So it looks bad for them to kill us in a city?"

"Yes, but out here it's ok. We have an hour before we are legally 'safe' in barbaric land. Soldiers will come for us soon." He stood up and placed his head on the tree behind him.

"Why are you sad?"

He turned to me with tears of anger, "Look at this! Our lives are over. There is nothing we can do now...! I hate life! It feels like evil makes up the backbone of the universe. Everything has corruptions! Human nature tends to make us do evil. Human society tries to put up laws to stop evil. But what we do is corrupt and outlaw goes against us; our laws judge us. What good is there in the world?"

"Max must have known this, but he still seen good."

Bryan looked up in anger, "Look, Max was good and it just seems the universe won't let him get ahead and change things. His attempt at fixing things didn't work and now my attempt failed. Evil just has a way of winning."

"We can still beat evil."

"How? How can we do this?"

"Evil hasn't won if we live. Until we die, evil hasn't won. We are barbarians now. If barbarians are still alive and if they need to have soldiers to go kill them; then evil hasn't won. If barbarians can live inside of a civil city then evil still hasn't won, it has a chance to lose. It's just in your mind."

Bryan let out a deep breath, "What now? What do we do?"

I thought for a moment, "Well let's try going to find a place to camp out for the night."

"And that helps how?"

"It's not like we can buy some food or sleep in a warm bed. We need to stay alive to win." I stood up and Bryan struggled with himself as he followed. We walked out and came to a river. Small birds and animals came and went. I turned to Bryan, "We should head down the river and see if we find anything interesting." Bryan's face was gloomy; almost like Max except his looked lonely and hopeless.

"Why are going here?"

"We need water to win. We just need a good spot for a fire and to make some small roofs we can sleep under." Bryan spoke almost grumbling, "The hours probably up. They should be coming soon."

"Then let's make sure they don't find us." We continued walking for several minutes. The land started getting flatter and the forest started getting thinner. We saw a sandy beach and an ocean. When we came to the beach Bryan collapsed to the floor. "Are you ok?"

"Well this is the end."

I looked around and off to the side was a crater, "we can make a home there." Bryan sluggishly picked himself up and followed. The crater was large enough for us to make a roof over it and still have some space to crouch under. Bryan just followed whatever I said. We found branches to lie across the crater and plant material to put on top. We couldn't find any food and the sun was close to settling. We crawled under when we finished and the sun finished setting. Everything was dark and cold. The only light was the moonlight seeping in from the entrance and our unprofessional handy work on the roof. I could see an outline of Bryan's face and arms. He somehow found a stick and rock without me knowing. He sat angrily striking the stick with the rock trying to make a spear. "What are you doing?"

"I'm going to give them a fight when they come get us."

I started shivering, "Are you going to get them?"

"No, I won't stand a chance. They are probably looking for us now. I just want to weaken them. They aren't going to kill me just like that. If they want to win they have to work for it."

I lifted myself off the cold sand, "Bryan, try to rest. Tomorrow morning we need to get food and water." Bryan didn't respond. I put my head down and started sleeping to the sound of Bryan's rock striking the stick at a steady paste.

A light flashed across my eyelids. I opened them to see the light flickering passed holes in the roof we made. I went over to see what it was; several shadows of men walked with flashlights down the beach. My heart raced as I turned to Bryan. Before I did anything I saw him sleeping; his face was angry and he slept with the spear. If I woke him, he might run out and commit suicide. If I don't we might not get away. I looked over at the hole again; the shadows were walking to us. I turned and crawled over to Bryan. There was a crackling sound on part of the roof we made. I looked up and seen four figures moving, blocking the light coming in from the holes. A voice whispered, "They are here."

I grabbed Bryan and tried to wake him up. He jolted up trying to fight and hit his head on the roof. "What happened?"

The lights flashing focused themselves on us. There was yelling, some thud sounds and a spray can. The light still beamed in but now it was dim. The roof cracked; Bryan got in a ready stance. The roof opened and hands came down to get us. The hands pulled us up into a cloud of smoke. The light lit up the smoke clouds. The hands that grabbed us belonged to four rough small men. They had beards and raggedy clothes. The men grabbed us so one held our arms and another held our legs. Bryan and I struggled to get free but couldn't.

I looked all around and seen shadows searching around in the cloud with lights. The men forced us into the woods and ran quickly. Bryan struggled and screamed. The men stopped for a moment and some got him to shut up. I bounced up and down while they held me. After a while I started to feel sick from moving.

The sun was coming up by now. We came into a camp; people were cooking with fires in small cans and fire pits. Their homes were small and were built up with sticks and leaves. As I looked around some people were wrinkly and others looked smooth. Some people were short and small while others were tall and hunched over. Some people had white hair and were losing it. One lady was holding the hand of a small soft midget. We finally came to this one place in the middle of the camp. It was a large open circle where all the homes were built around.

People started coming and gathered around the circumference of the circle. The men dropped us in the middle of the circle. I picked myself up and heard Bryan yelling at everyone. We were facing the same direction when a voice called from behind us. My heart stopped and Bryan was stiff. My eyes watered as I turned and saw Max. His hair and face seemed to be worn down by time and stress. Parts of his hair covered his face; the rest of his hair was longer and went down to the bottom of his neck. At all this, he still had a charm and a warm feeling about him. I walked up to him slowly. Bryan was sobbing on his shoulder.

Max spoke, "Guys we have work to do." Bryan backed up and we followed him to his home. The home was large enough for five people; in the middle of the room was a small metal bowl with a fire burning in it. Above that was a hole in the roof for ventilation; around the sides of the place were Max's belongings. Max walked behind the fire and sat down. Bryan and I sat with our backs facing the entrance. Max started speaking while some of the people from the crowd hovered around the room. "How were you guys arrested?"

Bryan looked at me then spoke, "We were looking for Nick at a party where there was illegal plants. Unfortunately, we got caught with the wrong crowd."

Max nodded, "We saw the plane drop you guys off sixteen hours ago. I wasn't expecting to see you guys come out of that. Where are Nick and Jesse?"

"Jesse didn't come with us and I have no idea where Nick went." Bryan paused, "Did you know Nick would keep doing this stuff?"

Max took a deep breath, "everyone is in control of their own lives. I can't make anyone do anything. All I can do is to give you a chance to do something."

I looked around the room, "What is this place?"

Max's eyes opened a little, "This place is some of the stories you heard about the barbarians. Anyone that isn't fit for their society comes here."

Bryan spoke, "Well where is here?"

"Well this place specifically is an island. They put 'barbarians' they find here so soldiers have something to do. There are three groups of us on this island, three different camps we can call home until they find it."

Bryan thought for a moment, "where is this island?"

"Not sure but there is land with a city a couple miles north."

I was curious, "What city? Who reported it?"

"It's a 'civilized' city for the adults who graduated. We send people on boats every so often so we can scout out what they are doing; and make our own plans."

"You're planning?"

"We want to end this. It's been going on too long."

Bryan looked back at the people then back at Max, "Your talking about?"

Max chuckled, "The problem isn't rules; The problem is what the rules are used for. You can't have any society without a structure and have some rules or a code of laws. Obviously stealing and killing for personal gain isn't right and something should be done. The problem comes when the rules try to keep people under control. The rules only apply to those who break them; and are only followed by the innocent. Lawbreakers don't care about rules and it applies only to them. But there is a bigger picture going on. The rules in our old home were used to funnel and control humanity. I'll show you soon." Max walked over to us, "just obey the rules simply morals for right now. Don't steal, try not to lie, respect everyone. If you do this we can get along for now. I need to worry about something; I'll be back later tonight." Max walked out of his home. Bryan and I followed him as the crowd of people started to disappear.

Bryan and I went off and started to look around at our new life. In one home a man had fish and animals laid out for sell. Across was a lady sitting on a dusty rug with fruit and pieces of metal and twigs twisted into some kind of jewelry. One spot was an open field with short, smooth skinned people playing some sport. Off to the side was a wrinkly skinned person writing on stones; teaching smooth skinned people. I came to one place where a lady was holding a small person in her arms. I walked up to her, "Why is this person so small? Is that a birth defect?"

The lady glared at me, "There's nothing wrong with my child!"

"This is your child? You people live with your parents?"

The lady laughed, "Yes, don't you?" I shook my head. She spoke with sorrow, "Why not?"

"I lived in a city and I never seen my parents."

"O I'm sorry. I was born out here and I gave birth maybe a week ago."

"But why is he so small?"

The lady laughed, "Well *she* is fine. Everyone starts off like this; over time they grow and get bigger."

I leaned over to see the little person. Her head was large and bold. Her eyes were closed and her mouth was wet. She moved her hands to wipe her face; her fingers were small and chubby. The little person was beautiful, for the first time seeing the beginnings of human life felt different. It brought a tear to your eyes and gave hope. Hope that one day this life can reach its potential.

A man called me over. I turned but I didn't know who he was. He came up to me, "Hello, I know your new and its close to dinner time. I was wondering if you would join me. Your friend will be there."

Bryan and I agreed and followed the man. We came to him and the man turned to us, "I am planning on making a stew with rabbits and vegetables."

Bryan smiled, That sounds different. I never had rabbit before."

The man smiled, "We need to get them." he took us around to the back of his home and he paused.

Bryan looked around, "What are we doing here?"

The man said, "They are in the pen." the man reached over a fence in the shape of a box made of sticks woven together with vines. Inside the box were rabbits all over the place. Some were large and others here were small and thin. The man grabbed some plant food in a bucket off to the side and tossed it in. the rabbits came over and he picked two up. "Look at this fresh meat. Would you two like the honor?"

Bryan and I looked at each other. Bryan looked at the guy, "What do you mean?"

The man held one rabbit in one hand and one under his arm. He walked over to a flat tree stomp and picked up an axe with his empty hand. "Would one of you like to do the honor?"

I looked at him, "Why are we killing it?"

The man smiled, "It's nice to have fresh meat."

Bryan tried to save the animal, Ccould we have a hamburger?"

The man gave him a strange look, "I don't have any pigs, only rabbits."

"What about venison meat?"

"It would take too long to hunt a deer. If you don't want rabbit I can prepare something else."

Bryan stepped forward, "Is this really the only way to get meat?"

The man knotted his head humorously. Bryan went over and grabbed the axe. The man held one rabbit against the stomp and then he called me. "Hold its body down for your friend. Good now you let the axe drop right here, on its neck. I'm not good with cooking with the head." Bryan lifted the axe nervously a foot over the rabbit. I looked up and moved my head so I wouldn't get hurt. Bryan hesitated for a moment then the axe dropped down. It got stuck in the stomp. The head rolled off and blood ran off the sides of the axe. Bryan backed up as I picked up my hands and looked at the drops that spattered on them.

The man picked up the rabbit and gave me the other one. He then tied the dead rabbit to a pole and dangled it over a bucket. Bryan looked at me and shook his head. I pointed to the animal and he grabbed the rabbit. I picked up the axe and looked at the rabbit. It was wiggling around and struggled. I positioned the axe in the right spot and got ready to thrust the axe downward. Bryan's face was blank. I closed my eye for a moment and took a deep breath.

The man gave Bryan and me some rags and we washed our hands in a bowl of water. A smell was coming from the house. The smell was one of the best I ever experienced, probably because I haven't eaten in a day. Bryan started talking, "I'm not sure if I'm eating."

"You ate stuff like this before you knew where it came from."

"Yea, but knowing now, I'm not too sure."

"You need nutrition from somewhere. I guess this is just a part of life we have to get used to."

"How can we get used to this?"

"Well I mean life isn't always comfortable. A price needs to be paid for everything. Nothing is truly free."

Bryan chuckled, "Air is free, I don't pay for that."

I smiled, "You pay the tree carbon for your oxygen don't you?"

Bryan smiled, "I guess; why is life like this?"

"Like what?"

"Why doesn't it feel like there is no way out? There is always something changing, always something being corrupted."

The man called us in the house, "The food is ready."

We walked in and sat around a small fire. His partner gave us bowls and some crude wooden spoons. They were carved out of wood. Over the fire was a pot with all the food simmering in it. The man pulled up a wooden ladle and poured soup into his bowl; next to him were two small girls and his wife. Bryan and I poured our own bowls. Chucks of rabbit meat floated on top of the broth. I tried eating, not thinking about it too hard. Bryan seemed to be sadder and sadder with each bite.

Max walked into the home, "Hey I need you guys."

We excused ourselves and went with Max. It was late in the afternoon. We followed Max and he took us to the woods with some other people. "Max, where are we going?"

Max turned to Bryan, "We are going see some of our camps; then I need to talk with some scouts that are off of the island."

I got Max's attention, "Why?"

Max turned as we walked, "Well there are some new people at this camp and it's also about time to check in with the scouts. I wouldn't go to send new comers normally; but because it's you guys and because they found something new, we are going."

We came to the other camp closest to sunset; their camp was larger than the other one. A man in a faded cameo uniform came to Max. "Good to see you; here is the news. Three new members were dropped off by plane. One is a girl and she has a cut down her leg."

"Is the cut stitched up?"

"Yes, before she was dropped off she was patched up. The only reason she's here is because we found the other people she came with."

Max chuckled, "Leave the crippled, great; we have some of those people. Where is she?"

"I'll show you." We followed the man.

Bryan got Max's attention, "What is your job here?"

"I'm in charge of safety and planning."

I started speaking, "How did you get this job?"

"Well they had one camp before and they kept losing people when troops came by. Every so often they would regroup and start over. When I came along I changed this. Now it's harder for the troops to find us and we lose less people. I started getting up special places that were harder for the troops to find and I had the idea of having smaller camps and better houses for this kind of life. Now we have a system that keeps us safe."

We came to the medical place; it was just a roof of different materials hovering over a hand full of medical beds and boxes of medical supplies. There was just one roof built over beds and boxes with many out of date medical supplies. We came to the bed with the person. I couldn't see who it was at first but there was a tall man hanging over a bed. The tall man stood over the person holding hands and smiling. Max walked up as I moved around the bed to see Rosella in the bed smiling at the tall man. She looked at Max then saw me off to the side. Her smile dropped and she called my name. I walked over slowly. She let go of the tall man's hand and reached out for a hug. I went over and the man stared at me awkwardly.

"I never thought I'd see you again." her voice was soft with a tone of relief. I came up from the hugs as there were tears running down her smile; "this- this is my father."

I reached out to shake his hand. Max walked over to the side of the bed, "I'm sorry to interrupt this. With your leg, how long have you had that injury?"

"Maybe a day."

"Alright; well we only have one doctor and three doctors in training and he bounces between this camp and the others. We can't give you anything for pain and if it gets infected there's only one option."

"I understand. I can suffer the pain, I don't mind it."

Max started walking off, "I'll be back." Max walked over to me, "how do you know her?"

"She's my partner."

Max smiled, "Nice to see you too are together; I'm going to find some crutches for her."

I turned to Rosella, "How do you know he's your father?"

Her father started explaining, "Well I work in one of the factories where we grow children to be sent off to the pods. We received recourses to start the incubation process then we gave each zygote a number and name. It just so happened that I was working with my own recourses randomly. That doesn't happen often."

"How did you end up here?"

"Well same way as you. I questioned what I was doing too much. A co-worker turned me in after lunch once. I remembered the name she was given and here we are."

Max walked over and placed the crutches next to Rosella on the bed. Her father and I both went over. Rosella stopped, "I got it. Back up." Max chuckled and put his hand on my shoulder. Rosella stood up straight and made her way to me. She put her arm around me for a hug while holding the crutches under her arm.

I hugged her as Max called me, "Sorry but we have to get moving. It's best for us to go on the boats with the cover of night both there and back."

Rosella let go of me as I went with Max and Bryan. Max took us and a small group of people back into the woods and then to a beach. Max and some of the other people went over to a hole with branches and leaves over it. They moved everything and pulled out two wide boats. Each one could hold up to eight people and had paddles. Max called Bryan and me over. We helped pull out one boat then pushed it to the water. Three other guys joined us as we went knee deep into the water. Max called us and told us to jump in. the boat floated and started to drift. The sun just set by now and we were rowing away from the island. The other boat was closely in front of us. After about a few minutes of moving the paddles back and forth we all took a break. The other boat threw a rope to us and a man on our boat tied it to the boat.

Everyone in the boat sat in a circle as the waves rocked us back and forth it was cold once we stopped rowing. No one talked much because we were all focusing on staying warm. I looked at Max who was to the right of me. Max had his legs close to himself hunched over with a pen and note pad. "What are you writing?"

Max saw me shaking and started taking off his rugged coat and placed it around me. "It's a sonnet."

"Your writing poetry now?"

"I just feel free now. What I write can't be held against me. My thoughts don't have to be confined to my mind."

"How does it go?"

"I'm working on it. I'll show you later." He stood up and we all went back to rowing the boat. I could already see the shore up ahead. We made our way over and pulled the boat up away from the edge of the water. We flipped the boat upside down then went up a hill off the beach. On top of the hill I saw a flat field, then off to the distance were rocks and hills, then a city in the background.

Max led the way and we went across the field. There was short grass growing; brown and shriveled up and patchy. I looked up and there were more stars then I ever remembered. Off above the city the number of stars went away and a glare was in the sky. Bryan started asking Max several questions. "So you said you're in charge of plans right?"

"Yes, I am."

"So what are you planning now?"

"Well, we first made a plan to try and get some people in the city to try and shut down the power plants. But something else came up."

"How would that help?"

"They would lose communication and have a harder time controlling people. While that happened we planned to pass out some fliers. Hopefully that would do something."

"Fliers?"

"Yea, it would question the people on everything they know. I mean none of them would believe the city could lose power; let alone by barbarians. That allows people to question."

I got Max's attention, "What came up?"

"We have one entrance into the city. It was an old part of the wall that cracked open. But they started to do some work outside the city near the crack. We have to wait and see what happens."

Bryan spoke, "How long?"

"However long it takes. Patience is everything; change can take a generation."

We came up to the rocks and hills and a man wearing a grass costume came up to Max. They started talking while everyone with us crowded around them. Bryan and I stood off to the side staring at the city. Max turned to us and handed us a binocular. "Look off to the side." He turned back to talk.

I look at the binocular and then looked at the city. There were fancy cars zooming around, but the majority of people walked. The people walking looked like they had smooth skin like the teachers at our school while the people in cars had smooth skin like students. Some people had on raggedy clothes and wrinkly skin. The people in cars had on suits and fancy clothes.

I turned and looked at one store. A man with fancy clothes and smooth skin stood in a window counting drops while a wrinkly skinned man mopped the floor. I handed the binocular to Bryan, he looked.

Max came over to us, "you're looking at the wrong spot. I was talking about outside the city." Max went next to Bryan and pointed. Bryan handed me the binocular; I saw several domes two stories high. Wrinkly people operated mechanics and built everything up.

We started heading back to the boats. I stood next to Max on the way back, "Hey Max."

"Yes?"

"Why are some people wrinkly and other people aren't?"

Max smiled, "See they didn't talk much about this when they taught us in school. Overtime our bodies break down and it's our skin starting to sag."

"So why do some older people have smooth skin then? Like our teachers?"

Max reached into his pocket and pulled out a drop. He held it up as we walked, "The biggest kept secret of our lives. If people knew, they would jump at it. If they knew the cost; that's different."

"What do you mean? It's just money?"

"What is this made out of?"

I looked at it and studied it just like I did years ago. We pushed the boat out to sea and we were in the middle of rowing when I finally answered Max, "It's a stone crushed with preservative fluid."

Max chuckled as he moved the paddle, "it's blood."

I jerked back unexpectedly, "It is?" The waves crashed up against the boat. The wind was colder and blew more than when we came out here.

"Yes, it's preserved in the casing."

"Why blood? Where do they get it from?"

Max spoke trying to catch his breath as we moved along, "Years ago they found out that a protein in blood could reverse the aging process. In some cases for hundreds of years if enough was used. Naturally everyone wanted it and went blood crazy." We stopped rowing and took a break. Max sat trying to be comfortable. "They tried extracting blood from animals but it didn't have the same results when crossing species. So people relied on donors and supplied it that way; the younger the blood the younger the results. Of course only the wealthy could afford this while the poor sold their children. Turns out this didn't work so they created the civilized campaign. It was a movement to try and have the young of everyone taken by the state to safely regulate and extract blood. Of course some people found a way to have it to their advantage. They started to regulate the population telling how many kids everyone could have. They had adults living in cities away from the younger generation out of fear children would be abused. Soon it came down to the fact that people wanted to live as long as they could. Blood became the currency in the black market and soon everyone used it instead of other currencies. They started regulating blood as currency from coming out of banks paying labors then from there it flowed into everyday life. Your youth and health are some of the biggest prices you can pay or at least one anyway. In the adult world they have personal machines used to open each drop. Eventually the more drops you had the more life you could give someone and the more you could live longer. Now this is where we are."

We started paddling again as I sat back remembering all the blood collections over the years. A pinch, every so often from us when we were in the virtual world. Every time we had gym; The blood test to see our purity; the test to see if we used any substances that would lessen the quality.

I made up an imaginary number in my head; one blood drawing would prolong life for two weeks. I then made calculations just pretending I could find answers. We had a blood drawing almost every week it felt like. We ate things that would help regenerate our blood. At one drawing a week for 52 weeks, I would have prolonged someone for 104 weeks, or two years. Let's say we do blood drawing for say 17 years; the 18th years- we graduate. That's 832 weeks, one drawing gives two weeks. Doing the final math I would have prolonged someone for maybe 32 years. Let's say 5 kids did drawing and one person collected from all of them. 160 years of life. Looking at blood drawing one drawing would seem like 10 drops. This means 520 drops per year per person.

Looking again one drop would be 1.4 days. A soda is one drop and a bag of chips is two drops. Paying in drops you give 4.2 days' up on life simply for soda and chips. So then what is life worth? We pay 4 drops for a steak, which is 5.6 days extra; is taking an animal, killing it and eating it really worth 5.6 days? Just a simple 134.4 hours? We pay 50 drops for a book; 70 days for a book? Is having the knowledge of math or a fiction story really worth 70 days of life? If someone had all the drops in the world could he choose who could have more life and gets to live longer than another person? Then it struck me again; let's say that a drop is worth 1.4 days. It could be really 2 days for a soda or even 10.

We came back to the camp Rosella was at, after hiding the boats. Max, Bryan and I came to Rosella sleeping in her bed. Her father was gone. "I don't know when she can walk." I looked at Max, "You are going to need a job of some kind for you and her. We don't have enough recourse's to just give away to those in need."

"So what jobs do you guys have here? Can I get one like you?"

Max smiled, "That's volunteer work. Bringing food home is your job. Make something and trade it for food, go picking or hunting. Whatever you want; we don't have a currency so just get creative and don't rip people off."

There was a rumble and boom that rang across the ground. Rosella jumped in the bed. I turned to Max holding my ears, "what was that?"

"They probably found us; we need to get going."

I went over and helped Rosella out of her bed. The three of us made our way into the woods, another bomb went off. I looked back and the medical area was up in flames along with some of the camp. As we made our way out we ran into other people from the camp that were fleeing. Up ahead we saw some of the fleeing people start running in our direction. Lights shinned from the direction they came from. Max turned to me, "Rosella has to hide." Rosella was half asleep and didn't seem to understand what was going on. Max pointed, "You guys might have to separate again. I'm sorry but we need to go."

Max went off with knowing. I understood what was next. I looked around at where Max pointed and seen a hole big enough to fit one person but small enough for someone to walk passed it. I grabbed Rosella's arm and pointed. She clumsily made her way trying to wake up and operate her crutches. There didn't seem to be any room for me so as soon as she was safe I turned. Before I could move, Rosella held my arm and pulled me in the hole. Somehow we both fit and she held me close closing her eyes for a moment. I moved my arms around her; the only things I could see was her head and some of the inside of the hole. I tried turning to see what was going on outside but I couldn't.

We laid there in silence for a whole. Footsteps came close to the hole and some ran passed us. I tried to look back but just seen dirt kicked down. Another foot went by and another. A final person passed by but after a second from them passing there was a scream and a thud. The person sounded to be in pain. I felt a presence and heard feet standing above the hole. There was a gunshot; the person in pain stopped making noises. I felt the presence move and dropped down just passed the hole. I felt Rosella hold me closer. The presence made some steps, then several other feet marched and moved on.

Rosella and I didn't say a word. After some time I felt Rosella drop her head back. I looked and she seemed to have passed out. I tried keeping her hair from touching the dirt floor. After an hour or so I started to feel tired. I closed my eyes for a moment, and then tried to open them. My eyelids felt heavy and they closed.

I opened my eyes and I was facing the opening to the hole. Rosella was sitting outside of the hole with her bad leg stretched out. She sat motionless. I moved myself and tried to crawl out. She pushed over for me to sit. When I sat up next to her I saw the forest around us in the daylight. Everything seemed beautiful. The light passing through the green leaves, the blue sky. The forest floor had brilliant flowers; the woods had a mystical look about it. A while away from the hole was the body of the person in pain. He was in a ball; his back was bloody with a shot through it. His arms were laid out awkwardly across his body. The ground around him was bloody with tree roots under him.

I sat straight next to Rosella. She turned to me and smiled, then held my hand. I smiled back, "Seems like nothing can stop you."

"I didn't really sleep for too long last night. I wanted to make sure we were safe."

"I thought you slept the whole time?"

"No I just closed my eyes for a bit. After a while it seemed like everything was safe so I moved you out of the way and made sure you were ok."

I picked myself up, "well we should try to find our way to the other camps." I helped her up, "there's another camp somewhere."

"I think I know where it is." Rosella led the way. Bullet holes were all over the trees; every few minutes we saw either a dead animal or person. For a while it was just us until we saw a man hunting. The man was from the camp we were heading too and showed us there. A doctor came up to us as soon as we came into the camp.

He took Rosella while Bryan came up to me. "It's good to see you alive."

He shook my hand, "You two, how did your night end up?"

"That was one of the scariest nights of my life. Soldiers were everywhere." His tone changed, "Max is hurt though."

"Where is he?"

"In his home. Come on I'll show you" Bryan waved his hand and we walk to Max's home. There were five men standing outside talking. I walked over and men stopped me. Bryan explained how we knew Max and the men stepped aside. We walked in and Max was lying on the other side of the fire pit. There was a man in a coat hovering over him. Bryan and I walked over. Max seen us and struggled to sit up. The man tried to stop him, "I'm fine, really I am. May I have a moment?" The man in the coat stood and walked out of the house. Max had his arm in a sling and dangled it from his neck. He had a cloth wrapped around his arm. "When people know your name and you have a doctor in training it's like everything you do can kill you."

I went over and sat across from him, "What happened?"

"Well I was running and one of the soldiers missed his shot. He hit my arm. I didn't notice until I made it back here. I almost bleed out apparently. Luckily the real doctor was in this camp. He said if I didn't have a drop in my pocket I would have died. He had to crack it open and put it in me. I don't know what blood type I am but I guess it worked. Look at this." He unwrapped the cloth around his arm. There were eight metal wires holding his skin together. "The bullet went sideways and sliced my arm. I kind of wish I had the bullet for show but; how did you make it?"

I started explaining, "Rosella and I hid together. A hunter helped us here this morning."

"I see, at least you guys are safe." Max wrapped his arm backup, "well I need to catch up on some sleep; I'll talk to you later."

Bryan and I walked out. The doctor in training seen us and rushed inside. Bryan went off while I went to see Rosella. She was in the house of the doctor in camp. I met her and we went off to try to find a place to make a home.

We picked a spot around the outside of the camp. I planned on making a house large and roomy. I went around and borrowed a hatchet then started cutting whatever I needed. Rosella tried to help me and I saw her struggling to pick things up with one leg. "Let me handle it, you'll hurt yourself."

"No I'm fine I can handle It." She went to pick up some large branches and tried dragging it with the crutches.

"Wait, why don't you pick some fruit or something? We need food and if I can get some water it would be nice." Rosella looked at me unhappily. After a moment she went off. She came back after two hours with a jug of water under one arm and small sack of barriers in the other. She waddled over to me, "What did you do?" I hugged her.

"I have my ways. You should know not to doubt me."

After a week our home was finished. Some of the people in camp said it was one of the best homes they seen in a while. Some of the people who lived there a while like Max weren't impressed. Three days after that the camp was under attack and we had to leave everything. Rosella and I found a good place to hide in for the night then spent the next day going to the next camp. We rebuilt our home trying to make it as nice and roomy as possible. Again after it was done we were attacked and had to flee. This happened several times over what felt like a few months; each time we rebuilt our home it was less and less impressive. After a while we stopped trying to make everything fancy and just made our home like everyone else. It was small but you could stand, walk around a fire and it was quick to set up. Everything we had we either carried it everywhere or it was something we were willing to risk leaving at home and having to leave behind. After three days of leaving an area it was generally safe to revisit an old camp to salvage things but it generally wasn't worth it. Every time we made a new camp Max would plan out where the next one would be.

Rosella and I were sitting next to each other in a doctor's home while he was checking on how her leg was doing. Max came into the house. "I'm going to have to borrow him for a few hours. I'm sorry he can't see you walk. But it's important; do you mind?"

Rosella looked up at him from the floor, "It's almost sunset."

"Yes, he will be back before morning, I will promise you of that. This is the only time I can take him."

Rosella looked at me then at the doctor prepping himself, next to her; she nodded. I went with Max; his arm was out of the sling but he still had cloth around it. "We need to go across the water."

"What for this time?"

"They finished constructing the domes and now we can carry out our next plan."

"I didn't know you had another plan."

"Yea I haven't had a chance to tell you. It's been a while since we last talked."

"It's not easy hunting for just Rosella and I on this island and definitely isn't easy with the soldiers patrolling. Soon there might be a famine; there just isn't as much animals around any more. I'm getting worried about what food Rosella and I can eat."

"Well we might not have to worry any longer."

"Why not?"

"Those domes are some kind of new technology; well, old tech remade."

"What do you mean?"

"Remember those pods you were in when you were younger?"

"Yea."

"These are those but on a larger more advanced scale. These are used to keep people alive in them."

"Isn't that what they did before."

"From what the scouts say they are some kind of Tim tech brand technology. It's the new thing in the cities." I thought to myself as Max spoke, "I was told in the cities they make smaller ones the size of a room for people to use; so they can escape the day and unwind to their own world. Seems like Tim was right."

"That's nice to see Tim achieved his dreams."

Max frowned, "It is but I don't think he was planning on what it would be used for. They are going to use them to see if there are any more barbarians. If the world a person creates isn't 'civilized' then they will probably come to this island. Some of the scouts say they even have to pay drops for their own world."

"What about the ones outside?"

Max started explaining, "The larger ones are for the people in control of the city. So far we know that a person can be hooked up to an exoskeleton on the inside. They could be fed drops and food and live there as long as they could."

"Why would they do that?"

"Well now they could live forever. We are passed simple drops; as long as whoever is on the inside can get recourses to themselves who knows what they could do. They will probably rewrite rules in their favor."

"All this just so they won't die?"

"What is death? Most people don't have an answer so they are scared of it. Now they can live and rule forever. They are probably going to hook themselves up to an avatar of some kind so they could interact with the outside world."

"If their leaders are outside the city can't we get them?"

"We don't know a way to them yet. The dooms could survive a nuclear blast if one happened. I'm not sure how they will get recourses but we will find out."

"So what now?"

"Tim wasn't the only one with a dream. Bryan's been one of the biggest helps to our cause. He found out we could hack the system with one of these new Tim tech stuff."

"Really? So we could shut down the power?"

"No, we will get into everything. We are hoping to hack the system holding the younger generations in the pods and change what they see. If enough generations come and go and the minority become the majority; the world can be clay for molding. The only problem is what to mold it to? How do we make a better tomorrow?"

We pulled out the boats just like before. Max didn't row because of his arm. He was struggling to write something. When we took a break I started questioning him, "what's that?"

"He looked at me, "o, I'm still working on poetry. It's been hard because I'm a lefty and my arm is kind of out of use."

"Is it done?"

"It's not perfect but do you want to read it?" he handed me what he had;

> When we reflect on all that, we call life
> And then we remember all of the pain,
> The friends, family, love that gave us grief
> And then all the dark times we sat in shame
> Then we all pulled a mask to hide our mood
> And when our friends ask we'll say we're ok
> And the storms of emotion always moved
> Around on our heads before we will say
> We let our lives go, as we followed
> Far down a path, we did not want to see
> Never questioning the lies, we swallowed
> Our ancestors willingly gifted me;
> An ungracious world of terrible fright
> Yes, one in which we live here tonight

Made in the USA
San Bernardino, CA
07 January 2016